Contents

	Editor's Note	09
	Preface	11
1.	Symbolism Of The Truth	15
2.	Symbolism Of Lord Shiva	25
3.	The Cosmic Dance	44
4.	Ganga And The Flow Of Knowledge	62
5.	The Third Eye	72
6.	Watching The Movie Of Life	94
7.	Transcending Duality	117
8.	The Open Secret	130
9.	Being In The Flow Of Life	142

SECRETS OF SHIVA

Also by Sirshree

Spiritual Masterpieces - Self Realisation books for serious seekers
The Secret of Awakening
100% Karma: Learn the Art of Conscious Karma that Liberates
100% Meditation: Dip into the Stillness of Pure Awareness
You are Meditation: Discover Peace and Bliss Within
Essence of Devotion: From Devotee to Divinity
The Supreme Quest: Your search for the Truth ends there where you are
The Greatest Freedom: Discover the key to an Awakened Living
Secret of The Third Side of The Coin
Seek Forgiveness & be Free: Liberation from Karmic Bondage
Passwords to a Happy Life: The Art of Being Happy in all Situations

Self Help Treasures - Self Development books for success seekers
The Source of Health: The Key to Perfect Health Discovery
Inner Ninety Hidden Infinity: How to build your book of values
Inner 90 for Youth: The secret of reaching and staying at the peak of success
The Source for Youth: You have the power to change your life
Inner Magic: The Power of self-talk
The Power of Present: Experience the Joy of the Now
You are Not Lazy: A story of shifting from Laziness to Success
Freedom From Fear, Worry, Anger: How to be cool, calm and courageous
The Little Gita of Problem Solving: Gift of 18 Solutions to Any Problem

New Age Nuggets - Practical books on applied spirituality and self help
The Source: Power of Happy Thoughts
Secret of Happiness: Instant Happiness - Here and Now!
Help God to Help You: Whatever you do, do it with a smile
Ultimate Purpose of Success: Achieving Success in all five aspects of life
Celebrating Relationships: Bringing Love, Life, Laughter in Your Relations
Everything is a Game of Beliefs: Understanding is the Whole Thing
Detachment From Attachment: Gift of Freedom From Suffering
Emotional Freedom Through Spiritual Wisdom

Profound Parables - Fiction books containing profound truths
Beyond Life: Conversations on Life After Death
The One Above: What if God was your neighbour?
The Warrior's Mirror: The Path To Peace
Master of Siddhartha: Revealing the Truth of Life and After-life
Put Stress to Rest: Utilizing Stress to Make Progress
The Source @ Work: A Story of Inspiration from Jeeodee

SECRETS OF SHIVA

Secrets of Shiva

By Sirshree Tejparkhi

Copyright © Tejgyan Global Foundation
All Rights Reserved 2019

Tejgyan Global Foundation is a charitable organization
with its headquarters in Pune, India.

ISBN : 978-93-87696-72-3

Published by WOW Publishings Pvt. Ltd., India

First edition published in March 2019

Discourses Translated by : Sunita Pant Bansal

Copyrights are reserved with Tejgyan Global Foundation and publishing rights are vested exclusively with WOW Publishings Pvt. Ltd. This book is sold subject to the condition that it shall not by way of trade or otherwise, be lent, resold, hired out, or otherwise circulated without the publisher's prior written consent in any form of binding or cover other than that in which it is published and without a similar condition including this condition being imposed on the subsequent purchaser and without limiting the rights under copyright reserved above, no part of this publication may be reproduced, stored in or introduced into a retrieval system, or transmitted, in any form, or by any means, electronic, mechanical, photocopying, recording or otherwise, without the prior written permission of both the copyright owner and the above-mentioned publisher of this book. Any person who does any unauthorized act in relation to this publication may be liable to criminal prosecution and civil claims for damages.

*To the Great Seers and Sages,
who unraveled the secrets of
creator and creation,
who encoded these secrets into
metaphorical idols and stories,
that future generations can
decode and benefit from.*

Editor's Note

This book is a compilation of discourses delivered by Sirshree over the years on the occasion of Maha Shivratri.

The discourses have been translated from Hindi, transcribed and compiled into chapters that address specific aspects of the symbolism of Lord Shiva. The conversational style has been retained in order to preserve the tone of the original discourses to the extent possible. The language may deviate from grammatical norms at certain places in order to preserve the intent, tone and depth of Sirshree's message.

The contents are solely meant for the spiritual growth of the readers. They are not meant to offend any religion, belief or lack thereof, neither to hurt the sentiments of any individual, group, sect, cult or society.

A QR code and short-URL are provided at the corner of the back-cover. The QR code can be scanned or the short-URL can be used in a web-browser to access a video of Sirshree's discourse on 'Symbolism of Shiva'.

Preface

A courier carries a parcel to be delivered to its addressee. The delivery staff takes care of the parcel, so that it should not be lost on the way to the addressee.

When the parcel is finally delivered, the addressee is amazed by the beautiful and shining wrapper and shape of the parcel. He shows it off to his friends and neighbors and showcases it in his living room.

One fine day, his friend suggests that he should open the parcel to check its contents. Though reluctant to open it as it would spoil the beauty and shape of the wrapping, he still goes ahead and opens it. He finds a chocolate bar and a soap bar in the wrapper.

He bites into the chocolate bar, but frowns that it doesn't taste like chocolate. He spews it out, only to find that he had not removed the wrapper! He uses the soap to have a bath, but the soap doesn't produce any lather. Again, he finds that he hadn't removed the wrapper on the soap.

You may wonder whether someone can be so ridiculous. But this is exactly what is happening in the lives of most of us. This story is symbolic and carries a deep message.

The wrapper represents mythological stories, traditions and rituals that have been passed on to us by self-realized souls and sages from ancient times. The wrapper is only important so long as the parcel reaches the addressee, i.e. the one who can unravel the mysteries within. The wrapper made up of mythology, traditions, rituals and festivals actually contains within it the message of the Ultimate Truth.

When Truth truly touches you, your life gets transformed. You will begin to revel in permanent and unbroken joy – joy that is independent of external situations. Life can abound in unremitting peace, love, creativity, and fulfillment, when you realize the Truth and get established in it. This is the ultimate goal of human life.

However, with the passage of time, the all-important message of the Truth has been lost, while the empty wrapper of traditions and rituals has been left behind. Man is focused on the empty wrapper of doctrines and traditions and lost the intrinsic message. The very objective of human life has been lost.

The chocolate of Truth can give true bliss, but people today are lost in its wrapper of superficial rituals. They expect fixed answers, fixed Do's and Don'ts for life's quandaries. Practicing these rituals will not bring real transformation. It is only when you go beneath the wrapper and delve deeper to understand and experience the higher understanding, that true wisdom can flower.

The soap of real spiritual practice can cleanse you, so that you rise above the grime and negativity of life and begin to experience life in all its splendor. But, we don't use this soap effectively. We get bogged down by the doctrines that surround the essence of these practices.

What is at the core beneath these rituals? What are the secrets of life, the secrets of the creator and this creation that sages have encoded into idols and stories? It is their creative attempt to convey the highest experience that human life is capable of. If we unlock this treasure trove of wisdom, we can move towards transformation.

Our external appearance is barely ten percent of our character; ninety percent is hidden within. However, in the case of idols that were designed by self-realized sages, it is the other way round. The inner character is depicted through various symbols on the external body. This is how you perceive the idols or images of God and decipher inner qualities – qualities that can raise man to the stature of God.

No amount of personification of God can help, unless it inspires us to change ourselves from within, unless they convince us to change our perspective towards life. Lord Shiva represents the highest form of symbolism of the Truth. Every little aspect of Lord Shiva's appearance and his stories are replete with lessons on molding and directing our lives to attain the highest purpose of human existence.

However, these truths, that were encoded into Lord Shiva's persona by self-realized seers have been lost in due course of time. On the occasion of Maha Shivaratri, people throng to temples, offer milk and *bel* leaves to Shiva, and then go home. Some drink hemp; some observe fasts. It is a task that they have to complete. They do it without even stopping to ponder why they are doing all this.

Some follow these rituals so that they don't displease certain people – be it Gods or their kin. The youth of today, on the other hand, will not do it at all, questioning these traditions and their practical utility. Some follow it blindly because they are told by their elders. Some do it for fun; for them, it is entertainment, a nice time to enjoy the 'prasad' and hemp. Some do it to break the monotony of their routine lifestyle.

But to derive the real benefit of understanding Shiva, it is essential to understand the essence behind his idol and these rituals. For that, you need to contemplate deeply, so much that you become one with Shiva. You understand Shiva, by becoming one with him.

The image of Lord Shiva and every story and symbol that surround Him is a blessing. Those who designed them have poured all the virtues of Shiva in one idol so that the future generations can decode the secrets behind it. Secrets that can be practically applied in everyday life; secrets that can raise the quality of our lives.

This book is an attempt to expound the secrets that are hidden in the symbolism of Lord Shiva. Beginning with the superficial symbols – the visual cues that one can derive from Lord Shiva's picture, it progressively delves into the deeper symbols that can lead you to question the very basis of life.

Contemplating upon the explanation provided in the chapters that follow, can deliver a paradigm shift in your outlook towards your own life.

1
Symbolism Of The Truth

There were two children. One of them had a book containing a picture of incense sticks. The other child tore out this picture of incense sticks from his friend's book and threw it away. Seeing this, the first child was upset with the way his friend had devalued his incense sticks. They started arguing.

A man, who was passing by, stopped to ask the children about the reason for their quarrel. When they told him the reason, he tried to settle their dispute, "How do you know that those incense sticks are actually real? You are arguing for nothing!"

The man tried to explain to both the children what really should be considered as true incense sticks. When the incense sticks spread their fragrance, when their vibrations are felt; only then they are real incense sticks. But if they are doing neither, then you cannot call them as incense sticks. They are merely pictures.

This is not just about children; in fact, it is more the case of grown-ups getting into arguments to prove that they are right. The symbols, which were mere pointers, have become a cause for arguments.

People use mikes to address large gatherings. Everyone knows what a mike does, but, what if the speaker's voice does not come through the mike? How can you call it a mike, unless voice comes through it?

It is not a mike when it is not working. When it is in action, it lets the voice come booming across the hall; then it is a mike.

Can a picture of the incense stick spread fragrance in our lives? No. Then why are we stuck with pictures?

Some of you may argue whether God is like that…like the picture that you see! But a picture is just a symbol. It is merely an indication, a pointer, but man tends to be confused. Why is he looking for a symbol in those pictures? Why do you need a symbol?

When you teach a child, why do you show him pictures? Because he is just a child, he is in kindergarten. He will comprehend and understand better with the help of pictures. A for Apple, B for Ball, C for Cat…

Likewise, we may make some pictures, some symbols, some paintings, a few statues and quite possibly some temples, places of worship. But then do it so long as the person in question is in kindergarten. But for how long will your perception be that of a kindergarten child?

If you want to gain a deeper understanding, then you must understand the essence that is being symbolized.

Now the question arises, can we believe in God if he is not in action in our lives? Has God been activated in your life? Has he come in action? If so, then accept him as God, otherwise don't. Otherwise, everything is just a myth.

When do you call water as water? When you see it in a glass or in a desert? How about when you see it in a waterfall; then what would you call that? A waterfall. Water is called water only when it quenches your thirst, otherwise it is just something in a glass.

Likewise, people who say that they believe in God, have half the truth. Similarly, those people, who do not believe in God, also have half the truth. Then what is the reality? We will be amazed when we try to understand it!

We may argue about the incense sticks and their fragrance. But the one that actually spreads its fragrance in our lives… only that one is perfect.

Some people are confused. But confusion is good. It indicates that there is a readiness, an openness to listen, to see life from a different angle. And it is crucial to bring the new angle as early as possible in our lives.

What is going on? First things first!

You keep thinking that first let my anger fade, let my desires wane off, let my depression come to an end, let my fears disappear, let my greed come to an end, and so on. Everybody is busy trying to resolve these issues. They, however, continue to be angry, continue to be afraid and still be depressed. If it is continuing in the same vein, then it means that nothing right is happening. In fact, the exact opposite is happening.

If we have the right understanding, then the rest will fall into place automatically. What should you do then?

First Things First

When a man is drowning and he swallows a lot of water, what do you do? Do you jump in the water, save him and start flushing water out of his stomach while still being underwater? No! You need to bring the man out of the water and then flush the water out of his system. Bring the man out of the water and then bring the water out of the man! This is the method. First things first!

The day you understand the importance of first things first, when you get the understanding and the immediate realization of the ultimate truth, you will be surprised to see how fast everything else falls in place.

Depression, desires…don't fight them one by one. There is no need to cut off Ravana's heads, one by one. Your entire life, you will be cutting off a head and each time a new one will grow in its place.

This process is endless. But as Vibhishana told Rama, if you destroy the core, the navel of Ravana, then there will be no need to cut off the heads one-by-one. You hit the core and the rest of the evil will get destroyed by itself.

Your head casts a shadow on the wall. Can you catch hold of this shadow? No. You can never catch the shadow. Catch your head instead, and its shadow is automatically caught!

Catch hold of one thing, which is within each one of us. It is important that you become aware of this one thing that is present in all of us. Nobody can give you that thing; it is already there within you. At best, what anyone can give you is an understanding of that which is already within you. The surge of happiness that you will experience after getting acquainted with that understanding will be immense. You will realize that you already possessed it, but were unaware of its presence, and that prevented you from enjoying it.

How can we bring happiness in our lives? First things first.

You might have seen that when a child sees something interesting, for example a balloon, in another child's hand, he immediately considers it as his own. He even snatches it from the other child. In his mind, he thinks of the balloon as his own and never even considers that he might have taken something that did not belong to him.

Now that same child who snatched the balloon, listens in a discourse that it is a crime to snatch things from others. The poor child goes home and starts wondering how he can stop himself from committing the crime? He will not stop snatching things from others, but now he is ridden with guilt as well!

There is guilt that, 'I snatch but I shouldn't; I get angry but I shouldn't; I have ambitions but I shouldn't; I have desires but I shouldn't; I have ego but I shouldn't!'

Earlier man had ego issues and was devoid of peace, but after listening to discourses, he has to also search for peace – another reason for restlessness. Now he is restless because he has no peace! So, then why do people go to listen to discourses if instead of finding a solution, they bring on more problems?

They have problems because they do not do the first things first.

No one can ask you to rid yourself of anger…it will go away on its own. Once you have the right understanding about life, about who you truly are, the anger will vanish by itself. It is the understanding that brings all the changes. It is important to be aware of this understanding.

Don't think that there is a man called Lord Shiva, waiting to do just that. Do you remember the images of Lord Rama and Lord Krishna that you may have seen on calendars? You will remember them as the actors who enacted those roles in TV serials. But they are just symbols or a representation of Gods. Likewise, these stories are symbols and not the reality.

The Loss Of Essence

Whoever designed these analogies and symbols did a great job. But then what happened over the way? People started worshiping the analogies; they started praying to the symbols! If we start praying to the stories that were meant to be just analogies, then what will the result be?

Some people keep repeating "Waheguru Waheguru". But what really is the meaning of Waheguru? 'Wahe' means path, 'guru' means someone who directs us on the right path. So then, Waheguru is the right path directed by the Guru for us to walk on, not just to chant. Why keep chanting it? It would be like someone chanting "MG Road… MG Road!" What is the point? One should walk the path.

Over the years, the meaning has been lost; all that is remembered is the repetition. All that was needed was to say 'Waheguru' first thing in the morning and then walk the correct path. But what has happened is that we keep repeating the same words over and over throughout the day without really understanding the meaning and without walking on the correct path. When will we stop repeating and start walking?

Man is very happy and content that now his life will be better because he has washed away his sins. What a beautiful word – Waheguru – and how it has been corrupted over the years! And it has not been more than 500 years when this word was used by Guru Nanak to direct Truth seekers. Then what do you think will happen to the wonderful and pious things said by Lord Jesus, Gautam Buddha, that were said thousands of years ago? What will really be left of it with such mindless repetition over the years?

There were some things that were just said and not written, so they have been passed over the years by word of mouth, from the guru to his disciple. They were passed down in a rhythmic form. It was easier to remember. If Kabir's verses were not rhythmic then they wouldn't have been passed down to us through the ages.

What has Kabir said in his couplets? If there were a recording system, he would not have taken the trouble of making the couplets. He would have spoken the 'truth' directly. As this facility was not there, he had to spread the knowledge through couplets. And it was through humming of the couplets that the knowledge was remembered.

It is easier to sing and remember the couplets as songs. Music is good for memory. The right side of your brain remembers music easily. Just like the film song that you hear seems as if it is echoing within you. For those who are receptive and attuned to discourses, even discourses would sound like music to their ears! Now if the discourses were also conducted with music, you would remember them. Music can be easily memorized as there is rhythm to it.

Kabir created his couplets because he wanted them to be passed onto subsequent generations. Today you are able to listen to those couplets, even though a lot of their deeper meaning has been lost over the years. Today people argue over the superficial meanings of Kabir's couplets; some say that Kabir meant this, while others argue that it was a completely different meaning. Even those who have conducted deep research on Kabir's couplets debate endlessly on the what they mean. However, these arguments and debates lack the essential experience of God. This is because those couplets that contained the core wisdom were lost in transit over the generations. Only those couplets, which could be understood to some extent became famous. The real couplets with deep meanings got left behind. But Kabir's, Meera's, and Guru Nanak's efforts were to spread the real message to the population because there was no recording system in those times.

Shiva – The Beauty, The Truth

Lord Krishna does not repeat the verses of the Bhagavad Gita over and over again for all the characters of the Mahabharata. He does not tell Duryodhana, "Rise up and fight, I am with you," just as he told Arjuna. It is risky to tell this to Duryodhana, for it would amount to telling him "You continue with your evil ways and I will stand by you." Neither does he warn Shakuni about the effects of inaction.

So, what does Lord Krishna do when Arjuna approaches him? He bestows him with divine vision. What does getting the divine vision mean? Lord Krishna showed Arjuna his true nature. You might wonder what is Lord Krishna's true nature? This is again symbolic.

Arjuna saw Krishna transfiguring into his cosmic form – Shiva. He became the essential truth. Because Lord Shiva is the truth. He is beauty and He is the truth.

Let us try to understand this. What is Truth, what is Beauty, what is this Shiva that Arjuna saw?

This thing that is within each of us is called Shiva, the Truth. He is the One that lives in each of us. He is the One that lives *through* us. The day we understand who we truly are, we will understand the reality.

Let's take an example of a man who has met with an accident. He has lost both his arms, both legs and both his eyes, he has lost a lot of blood and fresh blood has been given to him and he has been given an artificial heart. After all this is done successfully, if you ask him about his identity, he replies confidently, "I feel that I am still fully present!" Despite being physically disabled and incomplete to such an extent, when he is asked whether he is complete, he will still say that he still feels complete from within. Who is this within him that knows that he is complete? Despite losing so many parts of the earlier body, who is this that still feels alive and complete? It is this very Shiva that we have to understand within us.

There are several stories and folklores associated with Shiva. These stories are there to describe something important to us. They have a meaning behind them. Every appearance of God is a symbol of something. The idols of deities that you see, doesn't each idol represent an analogy? They are the result of the creativity of self-realized souls. Have you ever thought of it as a blessing? That this knowledge will continue to spread for several more centuries without any recording system? What was the wisdom that led to the design of these idols? What was the wisdom from where those analogies and couplets were created? What was behind those creations?

Idols were conceived by those who attained self-realization. To explain that experience fully, they would create a single idol with all the analogies included in it. So that when you look at the idol, each element would remind you of something. When you look at Shiva's eyes, you should be reminded of something. Everyone has two eyes, but few have that divine third eye, which is beyond the other two eyes.

The idols are a reflection of some deeper meanings. When Shiva's third eye opens, what does it reflect? What does it mean that he has held Ganga in his hairlocks? What is the meaning of the Shivaling? Why is Shiva shown seated on Mount Kailash? Why does he have a snake around his neck? Why is the bull Nandi sitting outside Shiva's temple? The rituals that we conduct on Shivaratri – offering milk,

Bel leaves…what do they really mean? They all represent something important and have a message associated with them.

Why is Shiva depicted as being placed below the feet of Goddess Kali? How would the meaning change if Goddess Kali was placed below the feet of Shiva? What is the meaning of their combination? Goddess Kali represents Shakti. Shiva is the origin, the foundation, on which the dance of Shakti is happening. So you see Goddess Kali arising from Shiva, dancing above him.

What is the reason behind so many different names for Lord Shiva? He has been named Bholenath sometimes, Gangadhar at other times! But what do these indicate? They are explaining different aspects through different names. Sometimes in analogies, there are many names to explain as many aspects just so that the focus can be directed to those specific aspects.

The basic teaching is being depicted in different ways by all the images; they all point towards the experience of self-realization.

When man starts thinking, he will discover barely a few things. But the moment he starts analyzing things deeply, he will constantly discover newer aspects of the knowledge…almost like the Upanishads! Every image will become an Upanishad. Every image or idol will be like a discourse that people will remember for ages to come.

What was Shiva's essence before the universe was created or before his dance began? He was silent. The third eye had yet not opened. As soon as the third eye opened, it triggered a series of events and each event was given a name. Each of Shiva's acts was given a different name by people. If Shiva is seated on Mount Kailash, he is called Kailashpati. He is a symbol of peace, so he is referred to as Shankar. Mahadev, the dev who is superior to all devas. How are these names given?

A god is referred to by so many different names, because he has so many virtues. Each virtue is associated with a name. People call him by the name associated with the virtue that resonates with them the most. They worship Shiva for whatever they appreciate the most or what is lacking in them personally. Some call him Bholenath because they believe that Shiva is innocent. While many call him Bhabhootnath because Shiva smears himself with *bhaboot* or the holy ash, some call him Neelkanth or the one with the blue throat.

The people who designed these images were extremely knowledgeable; scientists are beginning to realize this as they are discovering old civilizations at several archaeological sites. These civilizations were very advanced for their times.

It is extremely surprising to see that the inventions and advancements that we have achieved now, were already present in the earlier times! They created the same inventions and that too without the help of automation. There were no facilities for writing or recording, yet they displayed enviable creativity. They brought to the front those things that are needed for self-realization and we should consider that as a blessing.

But we need to dwell on the real reason why the idols were created in the first place. Each idol is a blessing and they should be considered as a blessing. Those who designed them have poured all the virtues of Shiva in one idol so that in future, when people behold these idols, they should be able to decode the secrets behind it. Not everyone may be able to understand, but there would surely be some, who would be able to decode these symbols.

Even if one person is able to decode the idols, it would be a great service to mankind. Whoever is able to unravel the secrets behind the idols can thereafter spread it easily to others.

■

2
Symbolism Of Lord Shiva

Our body, our external appearance is barely ten percent of our real character; the remaining ninety percent is hidden. In the case of idols, it is the other way round; the inner character is depicted through various symbols on the external body. This is how you perceive the idols or images of God and decipher qualities that are inner aspects.

If you look at Shiva's image, what do you see? The River Ganga is held in Shiva's hairlocks. How is his attire? Ash smeared all over his body, a scary tiger skin cloth, a snake wrapped around his neck and a third eye on the forehead. He holds a trident in his hand and he is dancing the spectacular Tandav dance.

The state of Shiva is one of serenity. How will you show the picture of a person, reflecting serenity? The moon on the head represents calmness and serenity. His eyes are half open, half closed. What does this indicate? It shows detached interest. Though he is interested in connecting with the world, it is yet a detached interest. The gaze goes outward, but is also focused inward.

Shiva is shown sitting on Mount Kailash, in pure white snow; so, he is cool and pure! The moon, Mount Kailash, snow, all of them are white, indicating a body with purity of mind! To hold cosmic energy, cosmic knowledge, one should be pure in body and mind. Otherwise, knowledge can lead to pride and arrogance.

Everything that is associated with Shiva's image is representative of something. Neel-Kanth, the blue throat containing all the venom, indicates controlling the 'I', the ego. The personalized 'I' is considered to be poisonous…everything that is impure is held in the throat, not allowed to come up to the head, nor enter the heart. How did Shiva practice this? By preventing the ego from raising its venomous head, holding it in the throat.

So those who have not researched, may immediately draw some irrelevant judgments on Shiva's appearance. But they do not realize that Shiva's appearance is a statement about how whoever conceived his image was devoid of all preconceived notions. Otherwise how else could man imagine God to be? People may wish to see a God, who is splendidly dressed, better than any movie star, adorned with ornaments that no one has ever cast eyes upon.

Man wants the God that he imagines to be spectacular, resembling none else. But how do you make an image that is free from any

outward assumptions? It should not reflect any preconceived notions through its appearance.

Preconceived notions make a person unhappy. The very idea of Shiva is to break all preconceived notions. For example, the preconceived notions of beauty do not exist; beauty lies in the eyes of the beholder! Isn't it?

People perceive what they see. Till now, it has been said that beauty lies in the eyes of the beholder. But thinking about this further, we will find that it is actually the beholder's preconceived notions that are beautiful or ugly. That is why, things appear beautiful or ugly. When there are no preconceived notions, then things are neither beautiful nor ugly, there is no happiness or sadness; everything is perfect beyond duality, beyond opposites.

Shiva's son, Ganesha, also does not follow any set beliefs. Ganesha's face does not resemble any pre-set notions. He has been made out of completely unmatched things put together. Almost as if he has been made out of things kept at home and this implies that God does not follow any set traditions. Even a child's scribble can look like Ganesha. Likewise, the Shivaling is also very simple, with no pre-set notions.

The Shivaling – the symbol of nothingness

Shiva represents the fixed constant; the center around which everything revolves. And the *Shivaling* is a symbol that represents the formless Shiva. There are vibrations everywhere. Everything is an ocean of vibrations. Amidst this ocean of vibrations, there is a center that is fixed. Just like when you look at the moving blades of a fan, you see its axle in the center, which is fixed and still.

All around your body there are waves. They are vibrations, an energy, a force. Why do we say Shiva-shakti? Shakti means energy. What is energy? The top part of the Shivaling, which is visible… that represents energy… that is Shakti. The entire universe is made of vibrations. This universal energy has been referred to by various

names…it is also called Reiki or Prana, or Metta, or Chi. Howsoever many names you might give it, they all refer to the same thing, the same universal energy.

So there is this energy within and around all of our bodies. Our bodies are also a gross expression of the same energy. Whatever can be seen, heard, or felt is this energy. And then, there is this fixed thing; the center of all of this.

Did you know that as much as there is the visible part of the Shivaling that protrudes out, there is also a part below which is not visible? The part that is not visible actually represents the formless un-manifested Shiva. That which is visible, on which you offer milk as a ritual, is not Shiva.

All these are just symbols. Even the offering of milk is a symbol. Why is that pot hanging on top of the Shivaling? And the bell that is hanging outside the temple? What is the bull Nandi doing sitting outside? All these are there for symbolic reasons.

The Shivaling appears round. Why is it circular? Because a circle represents completion, unbroken pure perfection. A circle is endless, it has no beginning, no end. This world was never born and will never die. People keep declaring dates when the world will come to an end. The dates come and go, but life goes on, the world continues.

There are cells within our body, which are made of atoms; electrons within these atoms revolve at high speed, energy is available for the body to function. If the electrons were to stop revolving, everything would collapse. At the center of every cell is a nucleus. At the center of every atom too, there is a nucleus, a fixed center. What really is the nucleus? The fixed center around which everything revolves!

The ling inside the Shivaling represents Shiva. Shiva-shakti is a combination. *Ardha-nareshwar* is a picture that symbolizes this combination of Shiva and Shakti. They are symbols. Actually, they are all within us. Nothing is outside. Everything is within.

There is a pot hanging on top of the Shivaling in which people offer milk and bel leaves to Shiva. What does this pot represent? It represents awareness. Milk is symbolic of the knowledge of truth. We are actually pouring the knowledge of truth with awareness. The path from where the knowledge arises and flows out is also the way for it to come in. This is an interesting fact.

If you are lost in a cave, how do you find your way out? You can light a matchstick and see which direction the flame blows. The breeze is coming from the opposite side and it is this side that you will find the exit from the cave. And the same would be the entrance to the cave as well. This is the understanding of truth from awareness. It arises from awareness and leads to awareness!

Under the visible part of the Shivaling, there is a plate or a saucer like surface. and on the right-hand side, there is a path for the milk to flow out. The milk flows in that direction. The right side stands for the right understanding, the absolute truth.

The pot is placed strategically so that the milk falls on top of the Shivaling. The milk flows over from the head till the base; it flows, thus sanctified, purified, from the right hand side. It is symbolic of our thoughts that travel from our head to our heart, getting purified, changing in their quality.

There are a lot of impure thoughts in the head – of falsehood, temptations, selfishness, of carnal desires – the head is swarming with all kinds of thoughts. But do they get purified by touching the heart? It is only with the touch of the Truth that the quality of thoughts changes; it is then that they come down to the heart.

Milk is offered to Shiva, which falls into the heart's cup. It is symbolic of people doing their actions with each activity representing an offering to the Lord. The milk being offered represents our actions. Offering milk that seeps onto the Shivling means surrendering our actions to the Universal Self, to God.

So you can see that the Shivaling is actually a powerful symbol. It is such a statue that connects both form and formless. However, it is nothing in itself. It is possible for man to dissolve his ego in this nothingness. When man surrenders to Shiva, he becomes one with nothingness.

There are hundreds of gods and goddesses, but with none of them is man so deeply connected as with Shiva. It is for this reason that Shiva is known as 'Mahadev'. There are several 'Devs' but only one Mahadev.

But for a 'Mahadev' to be made, there has to be a 'Dev' – a god – first. But god can be god, only if there are demons; and for demons to be there, man has to be there! Man is called 'man' when compared to an animal or *pashu*'. So animals have to be there. So for '*Pashupatinath*' to exist, pashu or animals and man were created when the universe was created.

And lastly, for the universe to be created, there had to be *shakti* (energy), which could not be possible without Shiva. In Shiva's absence, there can be no energy, then how could the universe be created? And we saw that Shiva cannot come into existence until there are the 'Devs'.

So do you see this circular pattern, and can you tell what was created first and what came as an outcome? This is just like asking what was created first – the seed or the tree? People keep going round in circles while trying to answer this question.

As long as you try to find the answer in words, as long as you search for the origin in your thoughts, you will keep going round in circles. This is why symbols are used to explain the truth.

Who were the creators of the Shivaling – this wondrous symbol of divinity? Those people who achieved self-realization and who were able to identify with the essence of Shiva within themselves. That is why they created the statue of Shiva and they blessed us all with their act.

Now when we look at the statues of gods and goddesses, we should remember that they are a blessing. If we accept this truth that each statue or image is a blessing, it would do away with most of the unnecessary battles that we fight in the name of religion. Man will understand that ignorance is the root cause of all evil.

If man would contemplate on Shiva's image and imbibe its virtues, he would realize the Shiva within. Why would he then break such a statue?

People, in their ignorance, criticize one religion in preference for the other, crack jokes on the expense of other religions; but they do not know that they are actually looking at the same thing from different angles. They want to watch the same movie, but one person wants to watch only the first part before the interval, while the other wants to watch it after the interval. Isn't it foolish to criticize one half before seeing the other half?

This silly behavior would come to an end when there would be respect for the creators of the statues. There would be deep reverence for the nothingness that is present in the statues, the formless that is present in all forms. In addition, even discourses and couplets would be venerated, because they are the ones that help us in gaining clarity.

What is the point of offering milk and the three-leaved bel to Shiva? It represents your mind, heart and body. We have to go from the head to the heart. Just as milk flows from the pot to the Shivaling, that is how thoughts should drop from the head to the heart and turn into '*amrit*' – the elixir of life.

Otherwise thoughts keep churning in the head and the heart remains a desert. We have to make sure that this does not happen. What will happen when purified thoughts are surrendered to the heart, to the Shiva within? We will be filled with happiness and then this happiness will overflow and radiate to everyone around us, just as the milk that is offered flows out through the saucer.

The Meaning Of Om

When we mention Shiva, we precede it with Om. What is Om? It is a vibration, a sound that reverberates throughout the universe. If you were asked to imitate the sound of a waterfall, how would you do it? Whatever sound you make to imitate how a waterfall sounds like, will it really be exact? No! There is no way of making exact sounds. But you can make a sound that closely resembles the sound of waterfall.

When you think of different religions – Hinduism, Islam, Sikhism, Christianity – all of them have the alphabets 'O' or 'M' in their prayers, be it Om, Ameen, Omkar, Amen or whatever…all have similar tones. They closely resemble the sound of the universal vibration. When you utter these words, they symbolize the experience of the universal vibration. It is an experience that is the same in all the religions. How? Because every human, who takes a dip in one's own inner Being, gets the same experience. This experience is possible only through the human mechanism. It is absent in animals.

Thinking about Om, one might be deceived that it is referring to the Hindu religion. It is not! It is just the beautiful sounds of 'O' and 'M'. These beautiful sounds are the very source of the words, 'mom', 'mother', 'ma', 'mummy', or 'ammi'. When you repeat the word 'Om' several times, it fills you up with its vibration; your entire body resonates with its vibration. However, within those vibrations, there is one fixed point. It is this very point that is referred to as Shiva.

Om is the primordial sound, the first sound of the world. When the Tandav dance of Shiva started, what was the first sound that could be heard in it? What was the first note? It is difficult to exactly describe the sound that originated from the dance, because it is beyond the grasp of our physical senses. The closest sound that our senses can fathom is that of Om. Om is also called '*anhad*' which means endless. It is a sound created on its own, as opposed to other sounds that are created by two objects hitting or touching each other.

The utterance of Om is revered because it is the closest way of expressing the experience of Shiva. The inner experience of life, which we call Shiva, is the *Anhad Naad*, which means that this experience is endless, eternal, unbroken, it is constantly going on without any interruption, without a beginning or end.

There is no need for using any force or interruptions. When we use force, there is noise. When we clap our hands, we use both hands and force; when we hit something, then also we use force and in both the cases there is noise. But there is one action where we use only one hand and there is sound. But this one-handed-clap is very different. It is the expression of Om. It is the ongoing endless dance of life. We need to get established in that Om with the understanding that the core point of Om is Shiva, Shiva is the essence. Everything else is a part of the dance, the energy that is emanating from Shiva.

The Importance Of Vibrations At Holy Places

Do you understand why people go on pilgrimage? What kinds of vibrations are there in and around those places? Do you feel like telling lies there? Why do you take off your shoes outside the temple?

There is truth in the temples and so you leave the dirt outside. Temples are meant to be places of purity. The places of pilgrimage are therefore places with good vibrations because people there always speak the truth. Words have power. Every word has a different vibration.

The mantras that people chant are all useless if they do not possess the understanding of what they chant. And if there is understanding, then there is no need for mantras! You just need to reach that understanding, get attuned to it. You need to acquire the knack of seeing.

Have you seen 3D art? You would have seen three-dimensional pictures or 3D stereograms as they are called. Initially, it is very difficult to make out a picture in them, because they are made of very small dots put together. You are told that there is a picture hidden within these dots.

Initially you may not be able to make out anything in the picture. But once you get the knack of seeing, once you get attuned to the picture, then there is no stopping you. You can immediately spot the picture once you get the knack of connecting those dots. When we get the knack of seeing what is always present but not obvious, we get attuned to it. Then we will never miss it.

Once we are tuned and can recognize the importance of the vibrations in those pilgrimage places, the next step thereafter is to understand how to adapt those vibrations in our daily lives.

There are positive energies in temples, in shrines and pilgrim places. The energies are from the prayers people have offered there. It is easy to experience the positivity or sacredness in these places. There is a reason behind the shapes of the temples and pilgrim places. They have domes where if you chant Om, the voice echoes back to you. Ringing the bell in the temple gives rise to vibrations of positive energy. These vibrations reverberate and return to fill us.

When we ring the bell in the temple, it is not meant for waking up God to tell him that we have arrived. On the contrary, the bell is rung to awaken ourselves! We ring the bell in the temple to awaken our own understanding and awareness of God. In that sound, we discover the energy waves that connect us to Shiva, to find the core, to rediscover the place that connects us to Him.

Why do we go to temples? Because, the greatest vibration is at work there. What is it? It is faith! Faith is the greatest vibration of the universe. You ring the bell to awaken yourself and activate faith.

Faith is already present within you, but it needs to be activated. How do people's wishes get fulfilled when they visit the temple? It may seem improbable. But it is faith that makes it possible!

But now, the misconstrued ideas about this are becoming a cause of blind-faith. Suppose you pass by a temple, and if you forget to fold your hands in reverence, you are immediately filled with guilt when you remember that you had forgotten. You feel that this will anger God. If you think about this deeply, you will realize that we have made up our God to be a very angry God. He gets upset at the very slightest mistake, like if you have meat on a particular day, or have a haircut on a designated day.

Everything was going good till the evening, but because you had meat by mistake, God will immediately get offended and punish you! We make Him out to be very fickle. He gets pleased very fast and angry at the slightest mistake. We have equated him to humans. When we get a promotion, we are happy that God is appeased and we feel dejected at demotions that God is displeased.

During Diwali, why do we pray to Goddess Lakshmi? Lakshmi denotes wealth. We pray to give respect. Giving respect to someone or something makes it grow. So will Truth grow, and so will understanding, when you respect and constantly remember it.

All these things, these actions and symbols are not for God; they are meant to fulfill man's life purpose. The symbols and signs have lost their real meanings. It is these very meanings that we need to find out.

Only one thing gives joy to God and that is when man imbibes His qualities and assimilates them in his own self. No offerings or actions can please God more than the fact that we absorb God's qualities in our persona. We need to understand this truth completely. Once every Shiva devotee understands this, he will give up maintaining the pretenses of outward appearances. Instead of concentrating on rituals, the devotee will concentrate on sincere prayer and remembrance of God.

The mind wanders and is constantly searching for something. But we need to harness its reins and concentrate on God. If the mind is concentrated on God, it will enter into deep contemplation resulting in understanding and assimilation of godly qualities.

God's images and statues are here to assist us and not confuse us. The earlier we accept this, the better it is for us in the long term. Otherwise, people keep getting confused. It is when we worship God with the right understanding that we will be able to connect properly with Him, with the Shiva within us.

An understanding of all these things will help us be His perfect devotee. As mentioned earlier, every leader should follow Shiva's guidance. This is because, with position comes power, money and these pave the way for arrogance. If the leader prays to Shiva, and views Him with the right attitude, he will lose his arrogance and overcome his mistakes. Shiva demonstrates that the role of the teacher or leader is to lead responsibly. It is the leader's duty to be the carrier of knowledge and to distribute it responsibly to all.

What kind of vibrations should surround us? They should be clean and pure. All the images of Gods have a halo behind their heads. What does it signify? It signifies clarity. The colors of the aura define the person's clarity of thought. If it is clear, the colors are bright and vibrant, whereas it is dull and murky in case of confused thoughts and constricted feelings. So the halo is symbolic of having clarity of mind. And what does it mean to have clarity of mind? Attaining the truth. And the truth is Shiva.

Attuning With The Vibration

In today's times, there are cameras that can detect an individual's aura. It is called Kirlian imaging. The Kirlian camera can capture the image of the aura around your body. The aura is the field of energy that projects around your body-mind. The energy level of the aura of every human being is different. The aura or the energy level when we are healthy is very different from when we are sick.

But do you know where the energy is most dominant in your body? It is your hands. That's why giving blessings has been considered so important since olden times. When somebody places their hands on someone else's head to bless them, it is a transfer of positive energy.

Even non-living things have their own energy, their own vibrations. During Dussehra, why do we worship machines? On the occasion of Dussehra, we pay respect to the machines that work non-stop for us during the entire year. Dussehra comes as an occasion to worship them and give them rest.

What do you do when you get a new machine – a vehicle, an appliance or a gadget? You welcome it with a little prayer or ritual. What are you actually doing? You are matching your vibrations, you are connecting with the machine and attuning yourself to its vibration.

You may have perhaps observed that a friend, who borrows your car or bike, comes back complaining that the vehicle broke down midway; the same vehicle that works like a song when you use it. If it never gives you any trouble, then why should it trouble your friend?

It has to do with whether you are tuned with the vibration of the particular thing. Even non-living things have their own vibrations and you need to connect yours with them to bring a harmonious outcome.

When you gain a deeper understanding, you realize that this entire world is one vibration, one energy. And the center of this energy is within all of us; this is the very thing that we need to grasp at the level of experience.

When you reduce the vibration of water, it turns to ice, and when you increase it, the water turns into steam. The only thing that happens here is the change in the frequency of the vibration.

Likewise, when the vibrations are poor, the human being is sad and sick. Change the vibrations. Whoever does this is beside the point…

the person himself or someone or something else may do it for him; but the vibrations need to change.

Why do shopkeepers always burn incense sticks before starting their day in the shop or why do dancers always touch the dance floor in reverence before a performance? They all do this to match their vibrations. You must have read in the scriptures too. Ram pays his respect to the bow before lifting it up to break it; Arjun pays respect to his bow before lifting it up to shoot the revolving fish in its eye.

Nandi – the Devoted Bull

What is the first thought that you get when you open your eyes in the morning? It is not about brushing your teeth, going to your workplace, bathing your child, or making breakfast. The first thought is the 'I' thought. "I am present, I am awake, I am" is the first thought.

After that comes "I am a girl" or "I am a boy" or "I am a housewife" or "I am the boss" or "I am an Indian". There are several offshoots of 'I' like "I am so-and-so's brother" or "I am so-and-so's father," etc. Then come the extensions to these identities. For example, with "I am the boss", there will be "this is my office" or "He is my subordinate" or "He is my boss." These are the branches. These branches just keep growing to form the mental world – the world made up in the mind.

The bull, Nandi, that sits outside the Shiva temple represents the human mind. Is he facing away from the temple or inward? Inward. He always faces the Shivaling. Why? Because, if we turn our minds inwards, the thought branches, which were growing outward, will also reverse and reduce in number. We will find that our thoughts reduce when we direct our awareness to the Shiva within us. The 'I' thought dips within and dissolves into pure awareness – the state of Shiva.

Inside our body-mind are the seven chakras (energy vortices) with a fixed center. This center, is beyond the chakras. It is this fixed center beyond the physical world, beyond energy, that we need to grasp. We need to realize Shiva through direct experience, not merely by our intellect or hearsay.

The bull, Nandi, looks inward into the temple, because if he were to look outward, he would see red clothes... sarees or shirts. And you know that red color drives the bull crazy! This is symbolic of the mind, because this is what happens with the mind.

It is the mind that wanders and then worries about irrational and unimportant things. "Why did this happen? It should not have happened like this"...and so on. Nandi bull is the symbol of our mind. If it were to turn inside, it would eventually become one with Shiva. The Nandi bull is an indication for you to turn the mind inward and dwell on Shiva, the Truth.

Like Nandi, we need to turn inward and practice Self-enquiry. Self-enquiry eventually will turn out to be Shiva's enquiry! Otherwise, being focused outward, the mind bull will be bothered with matters like the names of various visitors to the temple, their financial status, their social status, The bull will always be stuck in unravelling the answers to lame questions like these! If his focus is all concentrated outside, he will never be able to look within to find the answers to the real important questions. His focus will never get directed towards Shiva.

However, the bull is taught to focus inward. If he concentrates within, then he will see Shiva in his true, beautiful form. Shiva is the truth, he is beautiful and the harbinger of good fortune. Real beauty lies within, not outside. Nandi bull represents an ideal for the human mind; the ideal of being absorbed in Shiva within, instead of being focused outward. This happens only when the mind surrenders to Shiva.

But then how does one surrender to Shiva? The mind with all its thoughts, the body, the attention; how can all this be completely surrendered to Shiva? Nandi bull is representative of the mind that is attuned to the heart. Such a mind happily surrenders to whatever gives true fulfillment to the heart; it dwells in the heart endlessly. Nandi sits outside Shiva's temple, with happiness filling its heart, just looking at Shiva. It is through these signs that we have been told how to offer our prayers correctly to Shiva. If we follow these indications, we can get maximum benefit.

When we submit ourselves with right actions, we are churning the sea. We are making the elixir, the ambrosia, in the real sense and stopping the poison of negative thoughts in the throat itself. We are not letting the poison drop down to the heart. What is between the head and the heart? It is the throat. It is actually, the pathway between the two.

You may have observed that you like to make friends with those people who have the same qualities as you. Shiva, Shankar, is purity, good fortune, whiteness and He likes all these qualities reflected in the devotee as well. Shiva has His mind in control and He wants us also to have control over our thoughts, so that we experience the same pure happiness as He experiences with His pure and controlled mind. Those who are able to fulfill this desire are true Shiva devotees.

Bholenath – The Innocent God

Shiva is given different names according to His state of being, His abode and His virtues. Those who actually thought of the names knew why they were naming Him so, but with the passage of time and with usage, the names have got corrupted.

Now when He is addressed as Bholenath, people expect Him to grant their wishes at the earliest. He is '*bhola*' or innocent; so whatever you demand from Him, He will fulfill your wish. Whatever you desire, it will be fulfilled. But those who had named Shiva so, did not do it with this wish-fulfilling intention. People have derived their own meanings from Shiva's name according to their selfish priorities and requirements.

People do not pray in front of the Lord's idol for the right reason. They come to such a poor conclusion, that they would not focus on the right thing, which is important, but will do everything else.

For example, if someone buys a television, the right thing to do with it is to watch programs on it. However, they would use it for irrelevant things. What if someone uses it as a table, or hang things on it? They would just not watch programs or shows on it. That is why it is said, that the thing is being used for everything else, except that one use for which it has been made.

People expect Shiva to fulfill their own wishes, desires or fantasies. He is innocent, therefore they imagine that He will do everything that He is asked. But the people who had named Shiva so, knew that Shiva is innocent, because He is entangled in His own illusions. Shiva created the universe and then lost Himself in this dazzling expression. He is seeking Himself in His own creation. He is innocent and therefore enchanted and lost in His own creation.

It's like this example where a man records his own voice, "Should I come in?" And when he plays it, he genuinely starts wondering who is calling out to him! You would tell this man that he is a simple naïve man – a Bholenath!

Every name has a meaning attached to it. But more often, people use it for relief. People pray to some God and when their wishes are not fulfilled, they are told to pray to Bholenath who will fulfill their desires immediately. This is how the rituals also began. Shiva is considered to be just a wish-fulfiller. As a result, the actual meaning behind this name has been lost.

When you visit the temple of Lord Shiva, there is the offering of hemp. It is considered as Lord Shiva's favorite drink. People get intoxicated by drinking hemp juice. But what really is the hemp that is being spoken about there? It symbolizes the enchanting cosmic illusion. It resembles the tendency of Shiva to be lost in His own illusion, to be hypnotized, so to say, in the cosmic expression of His own Shakti.

The Significance Of Festivals

Festivals were created to remind us of all this. Most people will just celebrate festivals as a task and be done with it. They will think no more of them. They will go through rituals mechanically – visit the temple in the morning, offer milk and bel leaves to Shiva and then go home. It was a task that they had to complete. They did it without even stopping to think as to why they are doing all this. Some people will not even do that. They will just go through the rituals because of blind beliefs or even fear and nothing else.

Not knowing who might get upset, people repeat traditions just to keep the Gods and everyone else happy. The youth, on the other hand, will not do it at all, questioning the traditions and their uses. Some may do it blindly because they are told by their elders. Some will do it for the fun of it. They will do it for the tasty 'prasad', for entertainment, for the hemp. They will do it just to break the monotony of their routine lifestyle. "Whatever happens does not concern us, we will just go and visit the temple! We just need to do something different and that is why we will visit the temple for a change!" Some see temples as picnic venues. Many people visit temples just because it gives them a chance to travel, or because they feel secure in belonging to their so-called community.

But there are some who actually contemplate and analyze why they are visiting the temple and how their perspective will change after that. They analyze Shiva's idol so much and so deeply, that upon returning home, their life is transformed. They forget sometimes in between, but then the next festival comes as a reminder and they make it a point to contemplate upon it again and remember everything again. Festivals are here to remind us of the essence of life, to remind us of the Truth.

We should take this opportunity of Shiva's big night – the Maha Shivaratri – to understand his symbols and imbibe them in our daily lives.

3
The Cosmic Dance

Once there was a garden where some owls lived. One day a swan came to the garden and told the owls that if they took a sunlight bath, they would be transformed into swans. The owls had no inkling about the sun. They had never seen one before, the word "sun" itself was not known to them.

The swan told the owls about the sun, and about the day. So, the owls agreed to do what the swan had suggested. As soon as it was morning, the swan called out to them. The owls were filled with the wonder of sunlight for the first time. They basked in the sunlight and were able to see because of its light. They saw and they finally got a deeper understanding. They realized that they weren't owls after all!

Although this story is about birds, it is actually meant for humans. A story is always just a medium, an analogy. An analogy is a simile that is used to explain one thing using another thing of a different kind by comparison. For example, "He slept like a log". There is no connection between sleep and a wooden log. But maybe people felt that man sleeps like a log of wood, unmoved, when in deep sleep. So, this is an analogy.

Let's consider another example, "Sitting on a chair like a sack of wheat." Again, there is no connection, but when one throws a sack of wheat in a corner, what does one notice? It remains there in whatever manner it fell.

Analogies are used to adequately explain and effectively convey what cannot be directly communicated through words.

Maha Shivaratri is essentially an analogy. It is a way of describing what is happening, but which is difficult to explain in usual words. How to effectively communicate creates a dilemma and from this need arises a story, a poem, a prayer. Through these stories we get to know what is happening in the cosmos, which is indicative of what is happening within everyone. If we can understand these analogies, then we can comprehend our true self.

Thousands of years ago, Lord Shiva was alone and felt the need to communicate. When the world was not created, Shiva felt the need to communicate with Himself; to show Himself His own nature; to tell Himself about His vast potential. But how do you tell your own self about whatever is within you? There was no one else, with whom to communicate. Shiva was alone, and yet wished to express Himself, about Himself, to Himself!

Lord Shiva kept thinking about this, but then, one needs a body to think, and Shiva did not have one! How did He think then? How did He do it? He started to dance, the Tandav.

The analogy is not narrating a future incident, nor is it narrating a past incident even though the analogy starts with, "Thousands of years ago, Lord Shiva was alone... and then He began His Tandav dance!" The analogy is essentially trying to communicate what is happening in the present. It is indicative of what is going on in the backdrop of this cosmos, it shows how life is expressing itself. No sooner is the analogy grasped than it begins to have its desired effect in your life.

When you wave a lighted incense stick around in the air at top speed in circles, what do you see? All you will see is a virtual circle made by the burning point of the incense stick. The burning point of the incense stick is a very small point. If you swing the incense stick in a fast motion, then you can see a circle being made in the air.

The burning point of the incense stick represents Shiva in His original state of rest. When the incense stick moves, the burning tip creates an illusion of a circle. It represents Shiva in action. Shiva's original state is stillness, pure silence. But when this state expresses through fast movement, it manifests the universe. His movement and speed is like the fast speed of the incense stick in the analogy. This movement of Shiva is called the Tandav dance, that gives rise to this phenomenal cosmos. The world appears due to Shiva's dance.

There are innumerable details in the dance that Shiva creates. If you have seen the old black-and-white television sets, you would have noticed that the picture can be broken down into thin horizontal lines. But, these lines are created by a single point that moves at top speed. When you switch off the television set, the whole picture collapses into the middle of the screen as a point of light before the screen goes completely black. When this point moves with enough speed, the dance becomes visible and pictures start appearing on the television screen.

However, in that high-speed, if somebody were to ask you to exactly pinpoint the position of that light-point, to spot the position of Shiva in the cosmic dance, the burning tip, how would you show that? Where is Shiva's position in that circle?

The true form of Lord Shiva is visible when it is still and quiet, in the state of rest. The minute it started vibrating, the Tandav dance started. Then the cosmic dance is visible, but Lord Shiva is not visible. You cannot see the dancer, but only the dance. And what a dance it is! The dancer is lost in the expression of dance. Everybody will applaud at the dance, but the dancer is invisible. Everybody will focus on the incredible dance, but when it stops, where is the dance?

So, either the dance or the dancer is visible. Both cannot be seen at the same time. When it stops, then you can say that you can see

Lord Shiva, but then the dance is no more. It has disappeared. Is it possible to observe both simultaneously?

What happens when one meditates, and while doing so, shifts into absolute stillness? He is connecting with Shiva, understanding and experiencing the state of Shiva within himself. When he loses the sense of his body, almost as if the body is non-existent, he experiences the essence of Shiva. You do experience it every night in deep sleep as well. But in sleep, you identify with Shiva in ignorance; you are in that state, but you are not wakefully aware of that state.

So the question arises: if you move the incense stick at great speed, can you still spot the burning end? Can you spot the dancer in the expression of dance?

The dance continues, hence its sound continues; the vibrations arising from the dance continue. The dance is so graceful, with a lot of expression and feeling. Every aspect of the dance follows such rhythm and beauty that you are lost in the dance; you are spellbound by it. You can see only the dance; the dancer is lost in this expression.

Now, imagine that you are in the hall where the dance is going on. There are people entering the hall. Some have come before the dance started. Some arrived late. Those entering the hall were given instructions and were asked to spot the dancer's face in the dance. But the dance is so incredible and enchanting that it is difficult to focus on the face of the dancer. Those, who were present before the dance started, know the identity of the dancer. But those, who reached later when the performance had already started, are unable to detect the face of the dancer. The dance is so fast that it is difficult to identify the dancer! Some of those who came in late even refuse to believe that there is a dancer – they only believe in the details of the dance.

So how do you explain things to this person who does not know the dancer? This is where the Guru – the one who gave instructions – comes in. The Guru asks you to spot the dancer. Otherwise, you won't try to spot the dancer. The Guru explains the importance of shifting focus from the dance to the dancer and directs you towards it.

The mesmerizing dance continues. Those people, who had entered the dance hall before the dance began, have no questions and are enjoying the performance. They have no problems. There are those who came in just a little late, but understood the indications from the instructor and recognized the dancer. Even they have no problems. But there are those people who came late, and cannot recognize the dancer or the intent of the dance. They are confused. They can see the magnificence of the dance but are unable to understand who is behind it.

Till this date, these people's beliefs and assumptions about the presence of God have not been solved! This is because they are unable to see the Creator in the creation; they are unable to spot the Dancer of the cosmic dance. Even if there was one mistake or if the dancer stumbled even for a split second, then maybe they would recognize the dancer. But there is never any mistake and the dancer never pauses even for a split second. That is why they are unable to identify God, the dancer.

The one, who spots the dancer in the dance, revels in bliss. Everybody enjoys the dance, but there is one who enjoys watching the dancer as well. There is a unique overwhelming joy bubbling within him as he watches the graceful dancer. That is why he has a different smile from the rest who are enjoying the dance. The rest are concentrating on the beat, rhythm and the grace of movement – everything except the dancer!

But then, where is the dancer? The dancer that we speak of is not apart from us. We don't need to go anywhere to meet this dancer. The dancer is within us; the dancer is our very essence!

You can experience the presence of the dancer within you. It is happening within everyone. It is the source of boundless joy. All the minds and bodies are expressions of the same presence, but this presence is consciously aware of itself in some bodies, while it is unaware of itself in other bodies.

Celebrating Maha Shivaratri

If we start a particular task with lot of planning, but somewhere down the road, lose track of the plan or the reason for which we started at the first place, then no one will understand the reason behind our actions. We will keep asking others if they know the purpose behind our actions. Everyone will be perplexed and no one will know. It is just like a lot of people gathering at a place and everyone asking each other the real reason for their being together in that place. Our world has become like this.

Maha Shivaratri is here, but no one really knows the real reason for its celebration. People are asking each other if they know, but nobody seems to know the answer. The only thing they know is how to celebrate it – get up early in the morning, offer milk, bel leaves, drink hemp. People give up on their quest for answers after trying for some time. Someone has to remind them to renew their search for answers.

We need to understand the meaning of Shivaratri, so that we develop an understanding of all its signs and indications. We need to understand and structure our lives according to these signs. Otherwise, we may mindlessly keep repeating, "Shiva-Shiva" and reap no substantial benefit out of it. Chants may prove beneficial to some extent, but understanding the truth and then chanting can bring far greater results.

There are many beliefs associated with Maha Shivaratri. Hence, it is essential to understand whom are we referring to as Shiva. When at rest, Shiva is in his original state or essence; this was when the world had not been created. It is only when Shiva came into action, that the world came into being.

Shivaratri should be celebrated with knowledge; where we are able to identify the face of the dancer. We call it the state of Shiva-at-rest. We can achieve conviction of this state only when we delve into our inner being, when we seek our origin. So we have to return to our original nature. We have to return to Shiva within us, the point that gives rise to the circle of life.

The Shiva within us is connected to the "*shav*", the body-mind. Once the body is connected with Shiva, the Tandav dance starts and gives way to expression. Once we understand what is it that we are expressing, that is when we will celebrate Maha Shivaratri in the true sense.

But how will we reach that point. We can reach that point by dis-identifying from the body. We have assumed that "I am this body, I am this mind." We can dis-identify from the body-mind only when we shift our focus with the right understanding.

To be able to spot Shiva in the cosmic dance, you can coordinate or match your speed with Shiva just like two trains travelling along in the same direction. If you are sitting in a stationary train and another train passes you at great speed, you won't be able to see the separate compartments of that train. Noticing the faces of the people inside that train at this point is close to impossible. However, if your train is moving along at the same speed as the other train, you will be able to see the compartments, and even the people sitting inside the other train. If two trains were running at the same speed, then while sitting in one, it would seem as if the other train is stationary or not moving at all.

Likewise, you can witness Shiva and His qualities too. People who have reached this understanding of matching their speed with Shiva can see Shiva amidst His glorious dance and also appreciate His qualities. But then, it is not just a simple matter of matching speed with Shiva, there is more to it.

On the outside, you are stationary already; it is inside that you need to recognize Shiva and His speed. While the dance is happening at a dazzling speed, Shiva's speed is zero. The mind, which is constantly moving and agitated, needs to calm down and assist in returning to zero-speed.

This is an experience that cannot be understood by the mind; it cannot be experienced by thinking about it; it can only be experienced by actually *being* it. You cannot hold it with your mind. You will fail if you try to do that. Just like you cannot hold on to the burning part of the incense stick. You cannot count the lines of display on the television screen, let alone catching Shiva!

The mind cannot catch this experience, because the mind itself is part of the dance. You might try several techniques for this, but the experience will elude you. It is only with practice and meditation that you can learn to go beyond the mind and return to the stillness where the experience of Shiva exists.

Those who saw it from the beginning knew the dot or center from which the circle was made. It was just a burning point – the point of consciousness. When we call it a point, it does not mean that it is small in terms of space. It is a point beyond space and time. Space and time are born from this point, as soon as it began vibrating, as soon as the dance began. The action brought about an appearance of what we call the cosmos.

However, if the dance were stopped then what would happen? Whatever was visible due to the action would become invisible.

The circle would disappear once the moving action is stopped. Everything would vanish. The universe will also vanish and only Shiva will be left, in His original state of stillness. Shakti or energy merges back into Shiva.

With this understanding, you will be able to see and feel Shiva's omnipresence in the world. You will see everything and everyone around you, but you will be aware of only Shiva's omnipresence, manifesting as the vibrant dance of the world around you. It is these very vibrations that have created everything around you.

Whatever we are seeing, what is really behind it in the background? Who is dancing? Those who worship Shiva, develop faith in His omnipresence; they develop conviction in the play of consciousness. Whatever might be happening in the foreground, they are aware at all times of the dancer in the background – it is Shiva's dance for them. They are enjoying the performance, only because they have seen Shiva-at-rest. They have experienced Shiva within themselves, in the stillness that precedes thoughts.

Those who meditate can see Shiva clearly with their eyes closed. By seeing, it means experiencing Him, by being one with Him. Those who have experienced this life-altering experience know that there is always a larger dance happening behind all these dances that we see in the foreground.

It is just like when you watch a movie on the screen in the theatre. There is a screen on which the movie is being played, but you always know that the screen is permanent. The movie is a temporary movement, that appears because of the stillness of the screen. The picture on the screen should not be mistaken for the real thing.

The Dance Of Shiva

Shivaratri is celebrated every three months, but when it is celebrated only once a year, then it is known as Maha Shivaratri.

Have you ever wondered why it is named Maha Shivaratri (the Grand Night of Shiva)? Why was it not named Maha Shivadin (the Grand

Day of Shiva)? If we use the word "*Ratri*", then it refers to night, but that would be an incorrect reference to the occasion. "*Din*" meaning daytime, which is equally incorrect. What happened on this night?

What was the original state of God when the universe had not been created? Was it day or night? If someone were to ask you this question, you will not be able to identify it as a day, because then the sun has to exist. The sun did not exist at that time. So then how can you call it day! So, that leaves us with night, because that is the only thing present in the absence of the sun. When there is no light, then we call it "night". What is darkness? It is the lack of light. We need to give the lack of light a name, so we call it darkness; we call it "night". Otherwise, there is no night. But as we have to name the state that precedes both light and darkness, we call it "night".

Till the time the universe had not been created, for Shiva it was darkness. Which means it was "night" for Him. The "Grand night" or "*Maharatri*" came into effect or became known, when the universe was created, when Shiva came into action. He did a breathtaking and wondrous dance. It was so incredible that its vibrations gave rise to the world.

Imagine someone dancing on a stage in such a beautiful manner that things start getting lit up, certain things begin to appear around the stage as a result of the dance. However, as soon as the dancer stops the breathtaking performance, the things around the dancer become invisible again. Shiva's Tandav is the reason behind the appearance of everything. Suddenly, the darkness was lost. There was light and you could see the entire world. It is to remember this lost darkness that we celebrate Maha Shivaratri each year.

The Tandav is the Dance of Creation. Shiva has been picturized as Nataraja–the Lord of Dance. He is the source of the dance of the manifest world. Right now also, this dance is going on, but it is not the kind of dance that you imagine.

Shiva came into action. Parvati, Shakti, Shiva's energy, is the state of Shiva-in-action. In this state of action, He is also referred to as

Ardhnaarishwar or half-woman-God because of His oneness with Shakti. But due to ignorance, people compare the two and engage in debates instead of realizing the truth of their oneness.

Who is greater, Shiva or his Shakti? And to answer their question the best way is to ask them that when they see a dancer dancing, which is better, the dancer or his dance? The dancer and the dance are one. There can be no comparison between the two, because without the dancer, the dance cannot happen; and without the dance, the dancer cannot be known as a dancer!

Whatever we call Him, the underlying truth is: that which was at rest came into action. For example, when wind is calm, it is referred to as "breeze". However, as soon as it comes into action and gains velocity, it is called "storm". In reality, both are the same; just when it has a different appearance that it is given a different name. "Breeze" and "Storm" are the two names of the very same wind.

Likewise, looking at the universe, we should learn to see how this beautiful dance is going around us all the time. Few are those, who are able to see this. Don't think that the Tandav dance is happening only when someone is actually dancing. It is happening all the time, unendingly, continuously. Even if someone is sitting quietly, or if someone is meditating, the dance still goes on. When Shiva gets into action, that is when the universe is created.

Was it really a great night of joy then when the universe was created? People, who have not attained this understanding might reply in the negative. For those who have had bitter experiences in life, it would have been good, had the world not been created at all. But if the universe had not been created, then how would you even know if it was a good thing or not? You would have never known this, because to find whether it would have been good, the world has to first exist! That is why, it is a fortunate event that the universe was created and you need to appreciate this unique happening. It's such a wonder, but as it is an obvious happening, the human mind takes it for granted; and we stop seeing the wonder behind this creation.

Universe – The Real Reason

People question why the world was created? What was the need for it all? Man understands only the language of "need". Do whatever is needed, everything else is unnecessary. Now, what is the "need" for birds to chirp merrily at the break of dawn? There's no "need", it is just a spontaneous expression of joy. The language of man is carved around needs. Man doesn't understand that there are some things that are done just in joy. Joy is a precursor of certain things. It invites a good feeling. It is an expression. Happiness, in itself, opens up certain secrets.

Shiva started dancing, and the dance is visible to everyone now. But you didn't know earlier if you could see the dance. Did you? Mostly, when you walk on the road you can see the buildings, the traffic, the roads, but not the dance. However, if you have this divine vision, the perspective of this understanding, then the dance will be clearly visible to you. Whatever you see, is actually the dance, Shiva's dance.

Enjoy the dance but keep focusing on Shiva at intervals, because then you won't be trapped in any prejudices that bring unhappiness. It is such a wonder to watch the dance, what a sight it is to behold! Wherever you are, whatever you see, it's just the dance! You can feel the joy bubbling within you as you watch it and you have this irresistible urge to join in the dance.

Celebrating The Occasion In Right Earnest

We become true worshippers only when we imbibe the qualities of God and make them a part of our being. Every festival, birthday or celebration day gives us a reason to contemplate. Our contemplation should be so sincere and deep that it begins to reflect in the way we live our lives.

We need to walk one step at a time and with each step, we are that much closer to understanding the secret behind Shiva's essence. We will begin to realize the real reason for celebrating this auspicious day. For this, we need to contemplate on how to perceive the dancer in the dance.

We need to fully worship Shiva and contemplate on his virtues with the right understanding. Only when we fully recognize and value his virtues and attributes, can we imbibe those within ourselves. It is only then that we will become true devotees.

What kind of a day comes after the night of Maha Shivaratri? How will the world be perceived the next day, after celebrating Maha Shivaratri in right earnest? If there is complete understanding, one will abide in the essence of Shiva, the dance will be visible, the dance that created the universe.

If there is a glass of water, and there is a dance happening nearby. The vibrations that reverberate from the beats of the dance would create various ripple patterns in the water. As soon as the beats stop, the ripples stop. The water will be back to normal, calm and blank.

What did you understand from this analogy? That the dance's beats were creating a variety of design patterns. The designs of the Universe! The designs of ripples in water are easy to understand, but the patterns of the way life plays out are not so simple. We hold prejudices and biases against these patterns, without realizing that they are all part of the same dance.

Science explains it in a different language. Shiva's language is different. The only difference is in the language, and whichever language explains it best, that should be used. The important thing is to understand the underlying message and perceive the world accordingly.

Let's take another example of a road where there is a traffic jam because the road is blocked due to a herd of cows and buffaloes. It's a common sight in India. Now, ordinary people would get upset, they would get tense. But people who understand Shiva would say, "What a brilliant dance of Shiva this is!" They will look at the same situation differently. It is important to remember them as echoes of the beautiful dance! Then these things will stop worrying us. Those who keep remembering Shiva and His dance continuously, after a point do not need outside reminders. Reminders are required only as long as you do not remember what is important.

The Need For Meditation

Grief and pain remind you of a few things and you make them a habit. Old memories get revived and you start remembering things that you had forgotten earlier. This madness of the false personality that you have assumed as "I" brings grief and pain. Almost as if, somebody has announced that it's time for sorrow, it's time to be unhappy!

There is an announcement, "Huge discounts on fans!" Everybody runs to that shop because summer is here. As soon as the discount announcement was made, people rush towards that shop. But this announcement is like a "social pressure" because even those people, who had not really intended in the beginning or did not have the need to buy, will purchase things from the sale. Just because they see everyone else running to buy things from one shop, they also follow suit, out of curiosity and end up buying unnecessarily. Just because there was such a huge crowd in the shop, the others were also drawn to it like a magnet. These people think that there must be something important for such a big crowd to be there in the first place.

Likewise, what do you see in the world? Huge crowds of people are piling on the creations that Shiva's dance has created. The creativity needed to be praised; the dance is so impressive that beat after beat, it is creating something new continuously. A new thing is being created even before the previous thing vanishes. The scene is not vanishing, because the dance is continuous. If the scene were to vanish without being replaced with something new, man would get a chance, a pause, to question the validity of what he saw, but the scenes never stop. The only time it vanishes from sight is when man sleeps and is unconscious or unaware of things around him. But every morning, the same serial of scenes keeps playing.

In the unconscious state of deep sleep, people are not aware of the experience. That is why, there was a need to simulate a sleep-like state where one can remain aware – a kind of conscious sleep. And so, meditation was discovered as a way of achieving this required state of being. Those who found this way must have dedicated themselves to it for years together before they understood it.

Just like Edison discovered the way of making the electric bulb. He performed so many experiments, but failure did not deter him. Failure does not mean that you stop looking or searching. Those who discovered meditation must have tried it repeatedly before they found the right way. It did not happen overnight or by just sitting once. They tried and tried before slowly it started coming to them that there was a state where a sleep-like trance could be achieved while being awake. It is different from the deep-sleep, wakeful or dream states. They experienced something and continued experimenting.

In today's world, people keep experimenting to make new products continuously, because money is the motivation. The more the product is promoted, the higher its chances of success. The more filmmakers promote their movie, higher its box office rating and success. They use new technology, new this, new that! The money motivation is too much for people to really stop experimenting.

But what must have been the motivation behind conducting experiments on meditation? Once that secret is unearthed, then you will find freedom from all temptations. You will discover a new perspective towards your various aches and pains. You will feel free. Otherwise, you will always keep declaring that once this ache goes away, I will enjoy better. I will feel happier. It will always be…till I get a new job, till I finish this work, till I get promoted, till I get married, till I have a family…there will always be some clause holding you back from your happiness.

To add to this, just like the huge crowds in the shop draw others to the discount sale, people also queue in to buy sorrow! When they see others suffering in situations, they feel that it is normal to suffer. Parents inadvertently train their children to react with negative emotions. People program their own minds to react negatively and end up buying sorrow that they were never really meant to suffer, that too by paying a high price for it!

Everybody has many different thoughts in their minds that are holding them back from finding happiness. The need is to look for motivation that encourages experiments on meditation. Once that motivation is achieved, then there is nothing holding you back from finding your happiness. You will find solutions. This does not mean that problems will go away. They will come, but then you will see them getting solved, with solutions arising from inner peace.

The Deterioration Of Values

With this, you will discover the most important thing – that the "cosmic dance" is happening and it is on the beats of this dance that everything is happening within and around you. These vibrations are known as Shakti or Parvati, because we have the tradition of naming everything and giving it a form. With a personified name and form, it is easily remembered. If you call it just a vibration or a wave, it will be forgotten soon. So, Parvati then creates Ganesha. Essentially, the vibrations create beings or bodies.

This way, many images were created, but now there was a need to create the image that would explain the cosmic dance. But, how was that done? It was achieved by an image that was created from the combination of all other images. To make such a universal image, all other images were put together and the image of Ganesha came into being. However, there was no guarantee that it would be 100% successful but they tried. The intention was to create an image that was symbolically apt for those times.

But requirements and beliefs are constantly changing. What is considered beautiful today could be considered ugly tomorrow. You would have noticed that whatever was fashionable yesterday, people are embarrassed to wear it today. Beliefs are constantly changing. But why does this happen?

This is because the "agreements" are changing. This means that what people used to agree on earlier is now changing. People are associating their clothing style with social norms. A certain dress code means that the person is evolved and belongs to a higher class in society. So certain other dress code would be considered less refined. This is what the masses have agreed upon. It is not that certain types of clothes actually symbolize a higher class of society, while others do not. It is just that some people got together and agreed upon common standards and those very standards came to be considered as the norm. It is all about the belief system.

If tomorrow, by chance, a few people across the world came together and agreed that gold is not really an expensive metal; then the price of gold will drop. Some other metal, say copper, will be given more importance! People will divert their interest from their previous favorite gold, to some copper! All because everybody is in agreement that gold is not good any more.

It all depends on the preconceived notions of people, whether they want to be happy or unhappy. But then, there is always someone who questions the scale on which these things are evaluated. This results in setting up of new norms, discovery of new things, which people agree to look into and contemplate upon. Those who contemplate, appreciate the cosmic dance. They realize that it was meant for joy and not to bring sadness.

But then some people become judgmental. They start judging the cosmic dance itself. Imagine, they themselves are the product of the cosmic dance, yet they become judges of the dance. It is like children growing up to tell their parents where and how they are going wrong!

Unfortunately, people tend to fall in agreement very soon. If someone passes a judgment about something being wrong, they agree without much thought. They easily believe that the cosmic dance is not right, the world created is bad, so let's run away from it! And they go away to the mountains, become recluses, or then drown themselves in vices. Some fly up in helicopters and then see the creation below, and appreciate it – they didn't do so when they were on the ground and closer to the creation. Up close, they don't see anything, but from a distance they are full of wonder and appreciation for it.

Songs are being created all the time and there is always an audience for them. People are always moved listening to melodious and meaningful songs. They appreciate the beauty and the aptness of the lyrics. The benchmark of songs will increase or decrease according to their TRP ratings. The song that is a box-office hit, generates similar songs very soon. And unwittingly, each takes us away from the truth.

With every passing year, new beliefs are built and this has moved us farther away from the truth over the centuries. Lies have become the truths today. In the beginning, the effects of temptations and truths were at the same level, but now temptations have overtaken the value of truth. Whatever gained higher TRPs received mass attention and its copies were made on a large scale after its success.

So the announcement that was made due to prejudices was echoed everywhere, "What is the point of life? It should be filled with these many things, otherwise there is no point in living life." Man has taken it as the gospel truth in his mind and heart. It has become so firm in their mind-set that some people commit suicide while others go on a killing spree, murdering all those who did not abide by this rule.

Most of the time, you are under the impression that you are alive, living and working, earning a living, having a family, and that is all there is to life. If you are not dead, then this is all you need to do. Unfortunately, those things that were important have disappeared, with time.

But all is not lost! We should take this opportunity of Shiva's big night to understand its importance and imbibe His values in our lives.

4
Ganga And The Flow Of Knowledge

There was a king named Bhagirath, who is known for his resoluteness and perseverance in Indian mythology. He firmly resolved to bring Goddess Ganga on Earth.

Goddess Ganga is the symbol of purity; it represents transcendental wisdom that can absolve us of all sins, purifying everything that touches it. With intense meditation, penance, determination and perseverance, Bhagirath's herculean efforts were eventually successful in bringing Goddess Ganga on Earth to absolve his ancestry and future generations.

From Bhagirath's name, you can deduce that he is the one who drives his *bhagya* (fate) like a *rath* (chariot). He is the one who drives the chariot of his own fate. Bhagirath means someone who rewrites destiny with his will power.

What will those, who are entangled in the web of fate, do? Which Ganga will they bring? Unfortunately, instead of bringing the Ganga into their lives, they get washed away by the tsunami of life's challenges. They need to bring the Ganga, because it is pure, it is the ultimate wisdom. Only by wishing it so, the Ganga cannot be brought into one's life. It needs benevolence and determination.

Bhagirath did exactly that. He was a tenacious man who kept trying to convince Ganga with perseverance till she eventually agreed to descend to Earth from the heavens. However, Ganga warned him that if she descended, then the entire earth would drown in her turbulent water currents. He would not be able to save the world then. She put forth the condition that there should be someone who should be able to hold back and regulate the flow of the turbulent waters.

He now faced a new question: what could he do now? He needed to make sure that Ganga would not be the harbinger of destruction once it was brought down to Earth.

Regulating The Flow Of The Ganga

Bhagirath's efforts were to bring Ganga to Earth, but for such a vast and forceful Ganga to descend safely, there was a need for special arrangements. Ganga was no ordinary river to be brought to Earth. Will power is not the only thing that is needed. Along with it, the purity of the Ganga is also needed. To accomplish anything worthwhile, a combination of knowledge and devotion is needed. Without the other, they are both incomplete.

Ganga should descend to earth systematically. It needs a special arrangement. Hence, there was a need to take assistance from Jamuna. Jamuna represents stability, the ability to remain still. When the water currents are stabilized, then it becomes Saraswati – the ultimate wisdom that is bestowed in a systematic manner.

Not everyone can manage the force of the Ganga. So Bhagirath was told that the turbulence of the waters of the Ganga could be handled only by someone whose third-eye was open.

The Third Eye

Now, what does the third eye mean? It means the eye of understanding. One whose wisdom has awakened can control the flow of life's currents. What does having an awakened third-eye mean? This indicates one who is assumption-less, time-less, space-less, form-less, ego-less… a body where there is "less" attachment, where there is detached view. How do we depict that the flow of

Ganga is being regulated? How to connect a visual to this? How will people remember this?

So, you look at Shiva's image and see Ganga flowing from his hairlocks and you will remember that image! Lord Shiva bears the vastness of the Ganga and ensures that it flows in an orderly manner. Ganga is seated in Shiva's hairlocks but it must be distributed to everyone. This is how Ganga can flow for the wellbeing of everyone.

You can see the state of Shiva; how does it appear to you? He is the source of wisdom; distributing the Ganga of ultimate wisdom for the wellbeing of humanity. Ganga is seated in Shiva's hairlocks, so that it can flow easily for others in a controlled manner. If it were let lose all at once, then it would wreak havoc.

So, Shiva was chosen to handle this herculean task to save the people on Earth from being destroyed by the wild torrents of Ganga. Since Shiva's third eye of wisdom is open, only he could do this. One who can see beyond opposites, beyond duality, is the one capable of handling the force of Ganga – the ultimate wisdom.

Shiva can control the flow of Ganga because there is absence of any kind of prejudices, pretensions and assumptions in Him. Shiva is free from arrogance; the poisonous ego is held in the throat. It is from the throat that the sounds of "I, me and mine" come and that is where Shiva has locked them, without allowing the ego to corrupt the head and heart. Only that person who knows how to restrain and overcome his ego can control the turbulent waters of Ganga.

Shiva was the harnesser of Ganga; He knew the right amount to be released at the right time, withholding the rest of the rushing water within His hairlocks. If there were abundance of the elixir of life, what would it do? The Ganga that we get, should be made available to us at the right time, step-by-step, at the right speed. That is the reason why in Yoga, Shiva is referred to as the Adi-Guru, because He is the very first Guru of all. The flow of knowledge is being allowed only to the extent that it is needed and not more. And it is given only when the receiver is ready to receive it.

When Ganga is seated in the hairlocks and the third-eye is also open; then what will be going on inside the head? Do you think that the head will be filled with any thoughts other than for the wellbeing of others? If there are, then there will be absence of serenity. There will be tension and stress. So, Ganga and the moon on Shiva's head represent purity and calmness within – the state of peace beyond thoughts.

What is in it for us to understand here? One, who is unable to control the expression of his emotions and thoughts, cannot be the right choice for regulating the flow of Ganga. There are some people, who on acquiring knowledge, start screaming out from the rooftops, or dancing on the streets, proudly proclaiming their knowledge. This kind of an attitude is scary and deterring. It makes us feel that if this is what knowledge does to a person, then we are better off without knowledge! One should display the right encouraging behavior and control excessive expression. Looking at Shiva, one can easily see the reason why He is the seat of knowledge, because of His calmness and unpretentiousness.

Shiva is also called Gangadhar; the one who carries Ganga. He has the ability to do both – weed out the evil from life and fill in the nectar of life. Shiva's image explains this secret of moving ahead in a systematic manner very well. If you look at His image carefully, you would see that everything originates from the head. The moon also resides on His head. What does the moon depict? The moon is white and it depicts tranquility. Despite the power that He wields, Shiva is the epitome of calmness.

When one gains knowledge, higher status and power, it is extremely difficult to keep a sane mind, devoid of ego and pretensions. There is bound to be some arrogance that comes with all of these. However, Shiva has everything, and yet He is extremely simple, devoid of ego. He radiates tranquility around Him.

The Purity Of Ganga

What does River Ganga represent? It points to the ultimate wisdom, the ultimate medicine. Now what does the ultimate medicine mean? If you have a particular sickness, the doctor prescribes some medicine. For another sickness, you are advised a different medicine. However, when you take the ultimate medicine, you will never have sickness! If you do not fall sick, then what will you see in the chemist's shop? There will be just one bottle, containing the ultimate medicine, which will prevent you from falling sick. Other than that, you will not need any other medicine, because you will never fall sick. That is the ultimate medicine!

People drink the sacred waters of the Ganga as the ultimate medicine. They take bath in its holy waters to wash away their sins and remove the associated feelings of remorse and guilt, in the hope that these will be washed away from their life. They are sin-free as long as they are in the waters of Ganga, but the moment they come out, the sins get re-attached to them. Once they come out of the water, the dirt sticks back. You are clean only as long as you stay in the holy waters.

The wise ones, who came up with this practice of the holy dip, had a deep logic behind devising this custom. They saw that humans are filled with guilt of wrongdoings in their lives. Every person makes mistakes in their life in some way or the other and is constantly filled with pain and regret over their misdeeds. They are unable to lead normal lives because of the guilt. They are restrained by this feeling to even tread on the path of truth and purity. They are unable to move past their mistakes. And it is precisely for this reason, to allow them to correct their mistakes, to atone for their sins, that the idea of taking a bath in Ganga was initiated. Your sins will be washed away and you can start over afresh.

This is a very big thing – for a person to be able to atone for his wrongdoings and turn over a new leaf. Even in Christianity, they go to the church for penance; they confess and ask for forgiveness for their mistakes. By praying in the right manner, man is able to free himself of his sins; but is he really freed from it?

Over the passage of time, people have forgotten the true meaning of this ritual. They just take the holy dip and forget that it involves cleansing the soul too and starting over afresh with a new perspective and attitude. When you return home, you should be new, very different from the one who went to take the holy dip. If this thinking were employed, it would make this ritual an extremely pure and effective.

When you dip into the understanding of the ultimate reality, the ultimate truth, your sins will be washed away. You will rise above both good and evil. You keep getting stuck in the push-pull of heaven and hell, karma and destiny. Once you dip in the waters of the understanding of the ultimate truth, then you will rise above this push-pull. You will then laugh at yourself as to why were you stuck in them in the first place!

The Right Use Of Knowledge

Now that we have understood this analogy and the indications, we should become aware of our deeds. Shivaratri comes to remind us of this. Visiting the temple with bel leaves and milk is not enough. You will pour the milk on the Shivaling so that it flows from the head to the heart. The passage from the head to the heart needs to be cleared for the smooth, uninterrupted flow.

To be a true Shiva devotee, one needs to be in control of one's mind. The ego needs to be kept at bay in the throat, from where it arises. The personalized "I" is the poison that needs to be eradicated from our system.

When the seas were churned to get the elixir of life, the poison that came out had to be removed first. All gods and demons came to drink the elixir of life, but nobody wanted the poison. It was Shiva, who came to their rescue. He drank the poison, and left the elixir of life for everyone else.

Shiva's presence is the assurance of wellbeing for everyone. He will drink the bad and leave the good for others. Both the things are important. One needs to know both – how to distinguish between the poison and the truth. If one knows how to churn out the evil from something, then the ability to absorb the knowledge, the good, should also be there. Both the abilities have to be there, before the person can be considered perfect. Instead of just screaming from the rooftops about "What should not be done", one should also be able to tell "What should be done".

Shiva saves us from drinking the poison of the ego by giving us the wisdom of the true Self. But we are so used to drinking this poison all the time! Every time He saves us, we again search up the evil. It is at this time that we need Ganga.

The environment needs to be changed. Prisons were created all over the world to imprison the evil or wrongdoers. But this does not solve the problem. This is because, the mentality towards crime and evil is still there. People will soon get entangled in some new problems. Therefore, the capability to be able to hold Ganga in order to remove the poison and add the elixir of life should be there. When both the jobs are done, then it is a job well done!

We need to discover how to be perfect Shiva devotees. There is no point in trying to justify that you are not a Shiva devotee, or that your faith lies with Vishnu, Hanuman or Krishna. They are no different. They have been conceived as distinct images only to impart the same knowledge in distinct ways. It is important that we love at least any one of them, because love is that medium through which we can eradicate the poison out of our system. The important thing is to have some medium to remove the poison of ego.

People are used to drinking poison and tolerating pain unnecessarily. The poison of ego, which torments the human being. The poison and pain goes through the heart to the belly. Emotions like fear, anger, ill-will, guilt, and hatred wreak havoc on health. The important thing is to not just stop them from drinking the poison of ego, but to get them into the habit of drinking the elixir of life – the divine understanding of the true Self, the wisdom of Shiva. It is essential to replace the poison with the elixir of life.

What are people doing today? They are throwing out certain things from their system, but not replacing them with the things that they should be imbibing. We do tell children not to do this or that, but do we also tell them what they should really be doing?

Prisoners are locked away in prisons, but it is of no use, because they will continue to drink the poison there too. They get used to drinking the poison of hatred and resentment and find alternate sneaky ways of indulging in it. Is there any use of locking them away? If man is in the habit of vices, he will find ways of getting to it. It is an old habit. Even when everything is going smoothly and according to their whims, they will still complain. They will grumble about something or the other and feel sad. Why? Because, it has become a habit to complain and carry negative vibes. Man is so used to grief and pain, that when he does not have it, he will inadvertently go in search for it!

Shiva stopped the poison in His throat and gave the purifying waters of Ganga. He controlled the powerful flow of Ganga's waters, otherwise there would have been a tsunami of knowledge. People would have been unable to handle such a large influx of knowledge.

What does it mean to curb the flow of Ganga in the hairlocks? It means giving it a system; releasing knowledge systematically. Ganga would not be able to work on her own, she would need Jamuna as well. Jamuna jams the flow of Ganga's waters.

As soon as its waters are jammed, Ganga became Saraswati, which means, the knowledge provided in a systematic manner becomes useful. What is the use of having excessive knowledge, unless it is proving to be useful for its real purpose? People boast and claim themselves to be very knowledgeable. They recite couplets anytime because they know them at the back of their fingertips. They can even quote anything from spiritual scriptures. They are holders of qualifications, but on a personal level, they are the same as anyone else. They unduly worry about each and everything and carry pain within them.

Without internalizing, knowledge is of no use. It has to be imbibed to have a positive effect in our lives. The third eye has to be open. There has to be awareness to assimilate and practically apply the knowledge in daily life. Otherwise, it is of no use. Knowledge has to be sincerely used to explore the real underlying reasons for sorrow, which we are unable to see objectively when we are already suffering.

Grief makes the mind dull, weak, and sometimes brings the thinking process to a complete halt. Hence it becomes even more important to open the third eye – to observe from the third eye of awareness – when we are gripped by grief. The third eye needs to be opened in the present moment. It is important to remind ourselves that we are seekers of the inner truth. We need to begin introspecting our thoughts and write them down. Whenever there is time, read them, observe them with the detached third eye.

If this is done sincerely, you will be surprised to find that there was no reason for sorrow in the first place. You will discover that sorrow is felt because of baselessly believing the thoughts that arise within us, without really investigating them completely.

It is like someone who scripts his own imaginary story, creates characters in the story, and in the end, gets so involved with it, that he begins to suffer the pains of those characters for no reason!

How do you find relief? You just need to remember that you are suffering by your own choice, and it is not really required!

5
The Third Eye

You must have seen some 3D images where you cannot make out the hidden picture clearly. But if you concentrate hard enough and keep looking long enough, you will finally be able to discern the picture clearly. You find the point of focus. But if someone was to shake you physically or distract you, you will immediately lose the picture. Likewise, you need to stabilize your focus.

Once your focus is stabilized, you will find that you can spot the hidden picture very easily. You develop the knack of seeing it. It is then that you realize that the picture was actually not hidden… it was openly obvious. It was just that you didn't know how and where to focus.

Some people cannot remove their focus from their wish lists; there is always something more that they want to do for themselves. Some people are unable to focus their wandering mind. Those who do not know how to focus and meditate on Shiva remain clueless. They are only aware of themselves as the body or mind. They do not realize that the events that they experienced all through the years do not constitute life. It is actually what they learnt from those events that constitutes life. These people are not aware of Shiva, and therefore, lose the true experience behind those events.

They misinterpreted the dance as Shiva. They saw the world and mistook specific elements in that world for Shiva. It is only when you see Shiva constantly in this world, in the dance, that you have understood the true meaning. It is a continuous experience. Ideally, it should be that you look at people and events, but you see only Shiva. You cannot selectively see Shiva in one person but not in the other. If you are aware of Shiva and can see Him in everything around you, that is when you have the right focus. If it is conditional or selective, then there is a break in your focus somewhere. There is some assumption or belief that is holding you back from seeing the Dancer in the backdrop.

The third eye has not opened yet. The concentration breaks, the mind wanders. Shiva can be seen only with practice.

Half Open And Half Closed Eyes

If you look at Shiva's image, you will find His eyes are shown as half open and half closed. That means that meditation is going on. It is symbolic. When eyes are half shut, you have the option of seeing only those things that are needed to be seen. But then this means that there is a limitation. You can see either one thing or the other. In a way, it is good that you see only the good things and leave the unnecessary things unseen. All those irrelevant and unnecessary things that were visible earlier will now no longer have to be seen. Only the important and relevant things will be seen now. This is the external aspect.

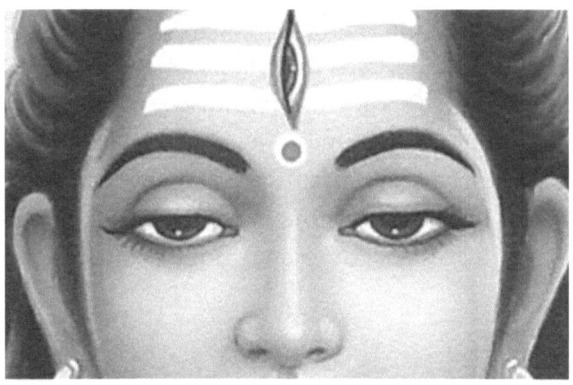

The eyes are half open, which means that things need to be looked at, as well as not looked at. You have to see the world around you, at the same time, not see it. If you want to stay detached and ensure that you do not get sucked into the world, get attracted to it, get entangled in the vision; how do you see things then? With half open eyes. This is the middle path.

It is not even correct to completely shut your eyes to the vision. That would be a temporary solution. We would not have come into the world at all if we didn't have to see it! Likewise, is the other option of keeping the eyes wide open. Have you seen how people open their eyes wide when they are watching an extremely interesting program on TV? Any kind of attraction, attachment opens your eyes wide. However, on the contrary, when you need to be detached, Shiva tells us to keep our eyes half closed.

How do we depict meditation externally? Where do we keep our focus with our eyes half closed? Those people, who are unable to redirect their focus away from the worrying things, lose their sanity and peace of mind easily. The same thoughts keep churning in their mind all the time. The problem gets magnified so much that either they need medical assistance or they end up ending their own lives just to find relief from their insane persistent thoughts. On the other hand, those who are able to redirect their focus away from disturbing thoughts, find peace and solace. One in a mental asylum, and the other in a state of bliss!

However, majority of the people are stuck in the middle of these two states. They fluctuate between finding peace sometimes and at other times losing all sanity. They continuously oscillate between these two states of mind. Sometimes, we don't even know if we really want to move away from insanity! We convince ourselves that if we concentrate on our own mind, which is pre-programmed, then maybe we will discover some new things or aspects. This is false hope.

Being Alone In A Crowd

We need to be able to be alone even while being in a crowd. Otherwise, we can be alone but still feel crowded. Crowded, because our mind is swarming with thoughts. We are constantly thinking of things, can see multiple things at the same time.

We keep thinking to ourselves, "He called me a vile name… that person is vile himself and not worthy of being my friend… that person was rude to me. Why did he call me a pig, why not a pug? Pug is good. He should have called me a pug." Our mind is constantly swarming with bad thoughts or good thoughts. We feel insulted if someone calls us a pig or a donkey. Why? Because there are beliefs attached to these animals. There are two reasons. One belief is that the donkey is a stupid animal and the other is that calling someone donkey is not nice.

How easily we feel slighted and upset because of these beliefs! How did the donkey become a bad name in the first place? If tomorrow some other animal was considered 'bad' then that will also become a belief. For example, if tomorrow, some person in anger called another person a 'camel,' camel would become a 'bad' word and 'donkey' will not. Our society is riddled with limiting beliefs. It is due to these that words take on 'good' and 'bad' connotations. We have to rid ourselves of these limitations.

When in a crowd, you are still alone. That means you are surrounded by people yet are alone, in the state of 'Shiva'.

Game Of Beliefs And True Happiness

Joy and sorrow are a matter of opinions and perspectives. Both of these arise due to the game of beliefs. Not just joy and sorrow, in fact everything is a game of beliefs! The day we understand that one incident evokes happiness in a person, while the same thing evokes sadness in another person, we will discover the truth behind shifting perspectives.

There is some assumption behind whatever is happening to us from morning to night. Every day we feel happy at some moments, then sad, then happy, then sad... have you been able to actually understand the real reason behind it? Have you caught the belief or assumptions that cause it? Or do you blame the world or situations for your woes? The day we understand this fully that we were basing our happiness on an assumption or belief, is the day we will become free. Free from the clutches of that perspective, we will laugh at the assumptions that we were holding.

In an India vs Pakistan cricket match, one player gets out. Some people will be very happy, while some will be heartbroken by the news. Why? This is due to their belief that they are Indians or Pakistanis, just because they were born in a certain geographical area on this earth!

We need to understand that this is all a game of beliefs. Are we going to cry over our temporary joys and sorrows that we feel due to these beliefs? The more we cry, the more there will be situations that will make us cry. So, we need to think deeply of the reason why this is so? When we contemplate deeply on our life events, we will be able to open our third eye and find true happiness.

The happiness that we feel once our third eye is opened will be immensely much more and also more intense than the happiness that we feel on petty or simple things. Nobody can destroy it or take it away from us.

We feel happy by being entangled in fake mindsets as well as when we are free of those shackles! But how different they both are! When we find true happiness, which is free of assumptions, it is permanent. You will still face the same challenges in your life; cricket matches will still be played, your favorite player will still get out; however, through it all, you will remain unfazed. You will remain "not out"! Nothing will trouble you. You will be free from everything!

Happiness is our original nature. We inculcate the habit of being miserable after a lot of effort. It is basic human nature to be happy, it is the original state, the state of Shiva; it is permanently within us. When you assume yourself to be something other than who you truly are, you lose your happiness, your original nature. Shiva was alone, and he was in immense bliss – so blissful that his dance created this phenomenal world! The art of being alone by your true self even while being in the midst of a crowd is very precious. Otherwise, people lose themselves in a crowd of incessant disturbing thoughts even while they are sitting alone!

Third Eye – The Understanding That Transcends The Perspective Of The Two Eyes

At first you may not even understand what kind of a God is this by looking at the image of Shiva, but you should be grateful that this image was drawn, where it was shown that there is a third eye. It is important to open this third eye sometimes and use it to view things with a different perspective. At least, when there is grief or misery, then this eye should be opened. You should open this third eye when troubling thoughts are draining your positivity and taking you away from your peace and happiness. It is the right time to open the third eye!

Shiva's third eye is the understanding that transcends the perspective of the two eyes. This implies that the third eye represents a perspective that is free from preconceived notions. This trait is not commonly found. The body that is genuinely pure without any beliefs is the one capable of receiving and holding the Ganga. There is suffering when there are preconceived notions.

Bholenath – Lost In His Own Creation

Shiva has been called Bholenath. *Bhole* means innocent or naïve, because He is. The one who gets so lost in his own illusions, and is unable to separate himself from them is called 'innocent'.

It is like this example where a person takes three to four voice recorders and records something in each. He records one dialogue in one recorder, the second dialogue in another, and so on. He fills in a lot of dialogues in different recorders and then plays them all together. It gives the impression of a lot of people talking at the same time with each other. It seems like one person is asking a question and the other is responding.

Whoever is listening from outside the room, will feel that the room is full of people having very interesting conversations. But when the secret is revealed, what will be seen? When that person will enter the room to find the source of all the chaos that he could hear from outside, to find the person who was narrating his sad story; he will find that in reality nobody was sad. On the contrary, there was nobody in the room!

Shiva is innocent and simple. He created illusions and got lost in them. He got lost in His own creativity, in His own compositions, just like a spider builds its web and says that it does not know how to come out of the web in which it is entangled. What will you say to that? What it has created, now it must un-create!

There is no web in reality! But then you are entangled, because of your own perceptions, your own beliefs and misunderstanding. You are trapped in the web of your own beliefs. Similarly, people have their own perceptions and ideas that limit them and entangle them in the web of their own making.

Man perceives the world and says sadly that things are not going the way they should be. Why did God create the world? It would have been better had He not done so. This seems very logical to a lot of people. But when these non-believers are made to deeply investigate their own inner truth, they will begin to agree. They will accept that they were being foolish and stubborn. They will then agree that God did a beautiful thing by creating the Universe. Their opinion changes once they introspect deeply. They accept that their alleged grief was a result of their misconceptions.

Will anyone believe if they were told that the sorrow in their lives was not a reality, but their own creation? They will immediately reject the idea and consider the thing that their mind firmly believes as the real truth. They believe that what came from their body was the truth, while the others were telling a lie.

The reason for all this is that man cannot separate himself from his own mind. He is not able to objectively look at the way his mind functions – the way it labels things, compares and judges people and situations. He gets caught up in the pain that he is experiencing. This is the reason why we say that man is very simple-minded and gets embroiled in his own beliefs. He is unable to objectively see the situation as it is.

Shiva is called innocent. Why? When people want wish fulfillment, instant gratification of their desires, they immediately turn towards Shiva. But over time, people have forgotten the real reason why Shiva is considered as the simple one. Shiva is lost in His own energy. Energy and power is created from a place of joy; the universe was created from limitless bliss. But that joy got sidelined over time, only power and energy remained of primary importance. The creation became important, while the Creator lost His own importance. Shiva has lost Himself in His own creation!

Journey Back To The Origin

What does the name Shiva mean? It means welfare of humankind; it means bliss. Shakti or energy arises from this bliss. This energy expresses and manifests as the universe. But in this expression, when the mind starts comparing and judging, it brings sorrow. Due to this, we forget our true nature; we forget the presence of Shiva and are lost in sorrow. We forget the purpose of this whole expression. We have to be then reminded of the omnipresence of Shiva in our lives. This is the journey back to the origin.

With every reminder, you are getting the opportunity to discover how the universe was created and how sorrow appears. How can someone get so entangled in the web of illusions they themselves have created? It can only happen due to lack of awareness. So whenever you find that you are getting lost in your thoughts and bringing sorrow, remind yourself about how you are so innocently losing yourself in the play of thoughts.

When you remember the truth about your oneness with Shiva, you are filled with joy. And the minute you forget how all this began, sorrow sets in. You have to give yourself a nudge of reminder.

The Power Of Thoughts

A sincere seeker of truth discovers how the universe was created; the very beginning, the eternal night, the state of Shivaratri, the state before the beginning of time. On seeking this truth, when the seeker has discovered all the secrets behind Shiva-Shakti, and still gets thoughts of sorrow, he is able to handle them better. It is the result of his seeking.

Without this knowledge, when one is saddled with despair, he becomes dejected; he immediately questions why only he has been the target at the receiving end; he feels that there has to be someone to blame for his sadness. He immediately shakes off all responsibility for his own condition, blaming someone else for it. Yet despair and gloominess does not leave him. He keeps looking for someone to blame, in the hope that his pain will go away and that he will finally find true happiness.

A normal person will think like this, while the sincere seeker of the truth will think otherwise. He will explore the reason for his sadness deeply, write it in bold letters and analyze it thoroughly. He will spend time in self-introspection, where he will contemplate the problem in such a way that if the same troubling thoughts were to come again in his mind later, they would not trouble him. There would be no feelings for that troubling thought anymore. The seeker makes space for only the truth and makes sure that there are no other feelings apart from the truth. If you were to do the same and not respond to anything other than the truth, just imagine what your life would be after that!

From morning to night, there are so many thoughts that arise within you. How many of those are thoughts of the truth? And how many of those thoughts are the ones that have no space in your lives? If someone were to analyze these thoughts to find out how many of these are the thoughts of truth; he would find there are some thoughts that give rise to the deep feeling of the Truth in us, while there are always some random thoughts that keep coming and going in our awareness. The latter ones are like clouds in the sky that disappear like the mist but make the sky look beautiful. These clouds do not affect the sky; similarly, these random thoughts do not trouble you, but you enjoy their presence in the field of your awareness while they last. Although they may be negative thoughts, yet you enjoy them. They come and go, but they do not affect you. You may wonder why? Because you have discovered the art of witnessing those negative thoughts with your third eye.

With the third eye, when you observe the negative thoughts that have the power to hurt you, the thoughts lose their power to affect you. Thoughts may still come, be it the thoughts of work, material stuff or any other desires, but how does Shiva witness them? With his third eye, the eye of understanding. You will be surprised to see that the same thoughts that used to bring negative feelings, do not cause such feelings anymore. This is true freedom.

Those, who could gain that third eye, the knack of looking at thoughts in such a way that they stopped affecting them; they could declare that they were truly free. Actions happen according to what is being seen on the clear screen. It is like travelling in the car of understanding, where the windscreen is clear. Where to turn or when to apply brakes is clearly seen, so no thinking is required. It is only when there is no clarity in seeing that thinking begins!

Action arises spontaneously when we are able to see clearly; and what is it that we see when there is clarity? We see that everything was created only for happiness; happiness underlies everything.

Seek And Ask

When you call a person a "soldier", then the word comes with responsibilities that a soldier needs to fulfil. He will have to go to the border, live in unbearable extreme cold or hot conditions, to protect and safeguard the country.

Are you a seeker? Just like the word "soldier" comes with responsibilities, similarly the word "seeker" comes with its own set of responsibilities, that of seeking the truth of life, seeking the truth of sorrow, seeking true happiness. So, whenever you have troubled thoughts crowding your mind, the least you need to do, is to seek and question.

You need to investigate the reason behind the pain. Do not believe everything mindlessly, with your eyes closed. Somebody says that they do not believe in life after death. Have they explored it yet? As soon as anyone is faced with this question, they lose their voice. Nobody can answer this. Nobody has researched this, yet they speak as if they know what they are talking about!

Drop Self-restricting Beliefs

Whoever developed these symbols wanted to depict everything. What is it that they were trying to show? They were giving indications of how to live! All the idols indicate the same things, because all humans have the same problem. Before becoming Mahadev, they became Dev (god), before that demon, and before that man. Who is this demon between man and Dev? It is the same old troubled mind that creates poison, the poison that is stored in Shiva's throat. The maker of this alleged poison is the painful thoughts of the human ego.

Everyone wants the elixir of life and not the poison. But Shiva gives poison, because the poison that he gives is not going to have any negative effect. It works as an antidote for the poison of ego. But someone, who holds the notion that poison is harmful, will suffer acutely when administered this poison. His beliefs will lead him to his death. With every cramp and every small symptom, even if that means a drop of extra sweat, this person will think that the poison is spreading in his body and slowly killing him. He will fear each moment and every symptom.

But with Shiva it is different. He holds the poison in His throat. Nothing happens to Him because He is sure of it. He does not have any belief that the poison will kill Him. It lies between His head and heart, in the throat, and yet nothing happens. But unfortunately, for people, they react in a different manner. Without knowing the entire story, how will they react? They feel, "Poor Shiva, He suffers for mankind!" But Shiva does not suffer. One who has no preconceived notions, does not suffer, not even by poison.

Socrates was given poison and so was Meera; Jesus was crucified; were any of them in pain or were they troubled? No. The physical body was wrecked severely, but they were at a level of awareness above the pain. The layperson does not understand all of this. They think that while Jesus was being crucified, with every nail, Jesus screamed out loudly.

However, Jesus knew that even if you throw a glass on the floor, it makes noise. The human body gives feedback in its own way; every system makes some noise when hurt. Likewise, Jesus must have been hurt while being nailed to the cross. But there was a clarity within Him that it was His body that was being hurt, not Him. The body hurts, not me. He liberated Himself with this firm conviction and that is why He did not suffer. Otherwise, it is these thoughts that convert pain into misery in life. You too will be able to store the poison in a detached manner, provided you understand that it does not have the power to hurt you.

Shiva is without restrictive beliefs. His idol also directs us to open the third eye. If people were asked to narrate their thought process, they would talk about their past, present and future thoughts. And most of the thoughts would invariably be of unhappiness. That is why, it is recommended to open the third eye to look at each thought objectively, without attaching emotions to them. The thoughts would then lose their negative power and would stop affecting you. None of the thoughts actually have any power over you, but they trigger emotions within you. These emotions bring pain and grief to you. Open the third eye and analyze those emotions, and they will disappear!

When you say that your neighbor is not a good man, have you actually investigated this carefully before making this statement? Have you asked his wife or his son about him? Ask his in-laws or his teachers at school. Maybe you will discover a new side to him! You might even discover that this person is worth placing on a pedestal and worshipping!

We should explore our thoughts and analyze them carefully before accepting them mindlessly. What kind of a habit is this to accept without questioning? Do we accept anything that someone else states without questioning their validity? No. But we easily succumb to our own thoughts, without questioning their validity, merely because of the assumption that if the thoughts have come from within our body, it must be true.

How does Shiva actually keep the poison in one place? Why doesn't He spew it out? It is important to know what is to be stopped or prevented from being expressed and what needs to be displayed or shared. Otherwise people are quick to show their anger but hide their love and affection for others. They do not share love and on top of that, they demand that they be loved!

Self-contemplation

You should try to rid yourself from restricting notions and analyze all those aspects that have particular belief structures attached to them. Write down these thoughts and introspect upon them, if possible give it the entire day. There will not be a lot of opportunities to do this during your routine days, therefore, try and do this at least on your birthday, once a year. But then what do you do till your birthday arrives?

Keep writing these kinds of thoughts. Write down all those sad tormenting thoughts that emerge through the year. This is not very difficult, is it? Write down every disturbing thought that you have. Somebody doesn't love you, write it down! On your next birthday, you can sit down to contemplate on all these thoughts and analyze them thoroughly. Nothing less than research and deep contemplation will work on this.

When you research on this, you may realize that you wrote all these thoughts in ignorance or due to lack of awareness of the full picture. The next time, you are plagued by the same kind of thoughts, you will laugh. Because post-analysis, you realized that it was just a limiting or invalid belief that had no basis and was actually irrelevant.

When you wrote that people don't love you, what did you find? You found that it was not others but actually you, who did not love yourself. One, who loves oneself, will not want to suffer even for a moment! These answers that you arrived at after contemplation are the answers that will become a way of life for you. If someone else told them to you, you would never believe them. These are important answers that you need to churn out from within yourself.

What did Zen masters do? They would ask their disciples to find out answers to riddles, such as how to clap with one hand? The answers that their disciples reached after deeply introspecting for months became a way of life for them. Because, those answers have come from within them.

Opposite Truths

In ignorance, you suffer even from the things that are not meant to make you suffer. Any sensible person would not want to suffer unnecessarily. It is common sense to question, why we suffer due to things that are not even meant to trouble us? Did we suffer unconsciously or were we consciously suffering? Upon analyzing, we will find that we endured pain unconsciously. It was an unconscious thought process. Just like some people have a habit of saying some words repeatedly, even if they are swear words. They become like personal 'catch-phrases' that we keep using repeatedly, unconsciously, unintentionally.

Likewise, certain thoughts come to you habitually, unconsciously. You want to stop the habit. You are a seeker, open the third eye because you are a true devotee of Shiva. Check how strong this habitual thought is. And you will realize that the truth is just the opposite of what you assumed. For example, you think that nobody loves you or pays any attention to you. However, it is the opposite that is true. You are not paying attention to others; and more importantly, you are not paying attention to your own self! You prove it yourself.

Love Yourself

When you self-introspect honestly, you will find that you do not pay attention to yourself. You ignore yourself. Had you paid attention to yourself, you would have known yourself well. Thereafter, it would not matter to you, whether someone pays attention to you or not, be it anyone. How can you expect others to do what you do not do yourself? It is extremely hypocritical to expect others to do things for you, that you do not believe in doing for your own self. Others would say, when you don't do it yourself, how can you expect us to do it for you?

Parents teach through example. If the father smokes and tells the child that smoking is bad for health, the child will agree only on his face but will continue the same behind his back. He will imitate whatever he sees. How can you expect anything otherwise? If you don't want others to behave in a particular manner, first ensure that you conduct yourself in the desired manner. Set an example and then expect it from others.

You will find that when you do it, you will not need anyone else to do it. If others notice and follow your example, that's a bonus. It will stop bothering you whether others are paying attention or not, because you yourself have gotten into the habit of paying attention to yourself. You have learned to love yourself.

Who Needs Make-up

Now we know who we are and what we need. Now we can give and fill ourselves unconditionally. Every second, ever day will be happy and beautiful because now we know how to conduct ourselves in the right manner. We were at fault from the beginning, but what an opposite answer we got!

You experience the Eureka! How does that happen? It happens when you explore. Everyone has his own journey of exploration. Everyone has different thoughts going on in their heads and hearts. Look around you. One person calls another ugly and says that the second person needs to apply make-up to look beautiful. But what do we find here? The second person is just like a mirror image of the person calling him ugly. It is actually the first person who is ugly, because he sees ugliness around him. It's like he's looking at his reflection in a mirror and telling the image to become more beautiful with make-up.

If you find a blemish in your reflection in the mirror, would you correct it in the mirror? Or would you correct it in yourself? Of course, you would make-up yourself, and the reflection will echo you. Similarly, the world is your mirror. Instead of spending efforts trying to correct the world, it is far easier and effective to make the corrections at the right place – within yourself!

Everyone wishes if only things would improve just a little more – if the wife would talk in a certain way, if the husband was to help a little more, if the children behaved a little better, etc. What is this, if not make-up? How do you perceive children? As angels or as monsters? If you feel they are behaving like demons, then they are actually reflecting you. If they are angels, then you are an angel too. They are just a reflection of you. This happens every day. Every day, you feel that somebody or the other needs make-up.

Dig Deep To Discover The Truth

Throughout the year, keep writing down whatever comes to mind. If you want to rid yourself of grief, if you seek eternal happiness, then it is important that you write down whatever bothers you. The sorrow will eventually be dealt with and removed permanently on the day you decide to spend time in contemplation. It will lose its power over you and will stop troubling you in the future.

When you think and analyze things deeply, you will be surprised that the only answer that you find is that you did not love yourself.

Had you loved yourself, then the fact that others did not, would not have the power to hurt you. It would simply not matter to you whether others like or love you or not. You would find happiness and contentment within you. If you love yourself, you would not live so long with false notions. You have been going about living your life with what is not true.

Post-contemplation, you will realize that you do not love yourself. What else do you find? You need the experience of love. But love is experienced by giving. You don't need to get it, but give it. You have a lot of love within you to give others. Once you start, you will learn the art of giving love, how to express it and what to withhold. It is important that you know both. You need to know how to maintain the crucial balance between the elixir and poison. You need to know how to perceive both joy and sorrow. With self-analysis, you will learn to explore deep within yourself and discover all the beautiful thoughts that are within you.

The disturbing negative thoughts that keep going on in the human mind bring with them the feeling of sadness. People keep thinking repeatedly: "Only if" my mother had loved me enough, "Only if" my parents had given me enough attention. They are always plagued with the "only ifs" and constantly live in the past. When you analyze it, you will unravel the secret that these thoughts that have been giving pain, are actually worthless.

Why should parents have loved you? Are you a beggar for love? No! On the contrary, you are the source of love! Thinking about it deeply, you will realize the futility of these thoughts and they will lose their power over you. Otherwise, the same movie will keep playing during the entire life.

How does the image of Shiva indicate all these things? How would Shiva urge you? By picking up his trident, he will ask you to gain control over your body, mind and intellect. The third eye has to be opened. Stories and folklore tell us how the third eye opens and everything gets destroyed! What does destruction mean here? It means destruction of all the irrelevant troubling thoughts.

Learning To Investigate

It is easy to explore, to find out why you are unhappy. We do everything only because it gives us pleasure, otherwise we will complain about why God created this universe! But have we really pondered over this deeply and researched on this complaint? If you explore this deeply, you will realize the futility of the complaint. If God had not created this Universe, then you would also not have known whether it was a good thing or bad thing. It was only after it was created that you could compare and complain thereafter.

Many times, when people ask questions, they feel that they have asked a very unique question. Nobody would have ever thought of the thing that they asked about! People with such thinking keep wandering around with worthless questions all the time, wielding them as if these unanswered questions were their weapons to prove their superiority!

If we are sad, then obviously, there is something wrong. This is the perfect opportunity to investigate deeply the deep beliefs attached to this thinking. Who needs to do the make-up? After all, the person standing in front of us, and upon whom we are passing our judgments is actually our own reflection! If we dislike the reflection that we see in the other person, then we should do some make-up on ourselves and that very dislikeable person will seem appealing.

When you make changes in your own personality, then others start appearing nicer and likeable. Then you will not hesitate to contemplate; you won't avoid contemplation with vague excuses. You will allow others more time and space for making changes because you are confident that after these changes, the world is going to seem much better and more beautiful. The key is to learn the right way to make-up.

Man does not have any big sorrows but only these little trivial things that need to be kept in mind. Since childhood, you have been used to a certain way of thinking and have a certain mindset. But now in adulthood, it is essential to make the change and opt for alternate ways of thinking. You may have been naïve and ignorant then and did not know the right way to think during situations, but now you are mature. You know better now with the knowledge that you have gained. You have the river of knowledge flowing in a controlled manner, thanks to the third eye of understanding! This knowledge should be utilized properly.

Third Eye – Purity Of Thought And Vision

The two eyes half open symbolize detachment. Whatever Shiva sees, He sees with detachment. Because being swayed indiscriminately by emotions is a cause of trouble; it creates unrequired bondage and that shuts the third eye. That is why the two eyes are half shut.

Then there is the third eye, which has purity of thought and vision. People's hearts are not pure. As soon as they gain even a bit of power, they immediately start plotting revenges and paybacks. This is not purity of mind. The real purity of mind is when it wants to spread the knowledge, to share the Ganga for the wellbeing of all. When we imbibe that purity within us, the whiteness of the moon; that is when Shiva will be pleased.

We believe that by offering prayers correctly, following the prescribed procedures with plants, milk, offerings, etc., we will be able to appease Shiva. But that's not it. Shiva will not be happy with all these pretensions. How will He be happy then?

You are most happy when you see the same qualities that you possess reflected in the other person's personality. Likewise, if you want to appease Shiva, then try and imbibe His qualities. Be immaculate and be good. Have clean and happy thoughts. The mental peace that one achieves after having peaceful and pure thoughts is indescribable. Try and bring that peace, accompanied with the meditative state – half closed eyes symbolizing a detached mind.

If you try and look at the world with half closed eyes, you will find a certain kind of detachment with things. Try it sometime. For example, when you watch TV with only half your eyes open, you will feel no attachment to what you see. On the other hand, when you are too interested in something on the television, your eyes will open wide. You are unable to tear yourself away from it. So detachment means half-closed eyes, whereas wide-open eyes symbolize attachment and involvement with things. It is an easy solution.

The next time when someone praises you, what happens if you half-close your eyes? There will be no problem. You will not get entangled in the web of praise. You will not make a rash decision nor get distracted from the path of truth. Shiva is, therefore, positivity, calmness, and purity of mind and thought. If the mind is pure, then it is in your control.

Love As A Medium

Why should prisoners listen to discourses while they are still in jail? Because when they come out, they should not spread the poison anymore. If the discourse is held in the prison itself, then it is necessary to spread the message in a conveyable and understandable manner.

Ask the prisoners about their beliefs. Whom do they have faith in? Someone who has faith in Shiva, will be explained through Shiva-based discourses. Because this way, you can have their attention. Otherwise, they will completely reject what is being said as sheer nonsensical talk. Likewise, some other prisoner believes in Ganesha and they are explained through analogies of Ganesha. The message can be conveyed through these channels of their liking and faith.

It will be extremely upsetting for anyone if they are told directly that they are ignorant. They will argue that their misdeeds are actually not wrongdoings. They just did what has been pre-existent in the world. If they didn't commit crimes, how would they be able to eradicate the bad people?

On interviewing each prisoner separately, different viewpoints will be revealed. They will present their own stories. Bringing these stories to light will reveal the need for them to look beyond their stories. If four people get together to read these stories, it does not automatically mean that these stories are authentic and are the ultimate truths!

These people are unaware that they are bound by their own stories. When they are listening to your stories, then they are actually concentrating on their own stories. They are not really listening to you. They are hearing what they want to hear. That is why, it is important to teach them what they really should hear. Everyone has to understand how to listen.

Shivaratri is a good time to listen, understand the use of the third eye to see things more deeply, to gain that perspective that transcends all beliefs. Shiva's dance helps us discover His creation. His image helps us to perceive and understand our inner selves, getting rid of all our preconceived notions.

Shav And Shiva

There is only Shiva and nothing else. The dance is happening only due to the one Dancer; we might as well learn to enjoy it.

Consider a man who suffers a terrible accident and undergoes major blood loss as a result. So almost all of his blood is changed, his body parts that were broken are now replaced with prosthetic replacements. Yet, he considers himself as complete. On being asked if he feels incomplete or half, since most of his blood and body parts have been replaced; his response is a vehement denial. He feels he is still the same since whatever happened was with his outer *shav* or the body but his inner 'Shiva' is still intact.

It is to discover this very difference between the *shav* (body) and Shiva that worship is done. It is very important to be always aware of this difference. Those who do not understand, confuse the body with Shiva and become the possessor of unnecessary and unrequired pride.

The body gets promoted to a higher position and becomes arrogant. What about the 'real' Shiva? He has no pride or vanity, but just plain purity of mind. How do we know that? His head is adorned with the cool waters of river Ganga and the moon. What do the moon and the snow of Mount Kailash indicate? They represent coolness, whiteness, the calmness and purity of mind.

Glasses Of Joy

All these things that we are discussing are due to the medium of Shiva. If you are a Shiva devotee, you will pay attention to what is being said here. But actually the work to be done is the same, irrespective of whom you worship. There is only one important thing and that is to liberate ourselves of grief and pain.

We are suffering unnecessarily. The heart may refuse to accept this but we have to convince ourselves that our suffering is futile and pointless. Investigate sincerely and you will find yourself to always be in the same condition wherever you might be; be it in a crowd or alone in a forest.

Investigate with love and kindness. It will not hurt. It becomes more appealing to make an effort because we love Shiva. With this thought in mind, you can be calmer and like a true Shiva devotee, you can explore your thoughts deeply. Situations will then stop bothering you. You will constantly be in a state of happiness.

Constantly wear your glasses of happiness irrespective of whatever incidents are occurring around you. Beliefs interrupt your happiness. Keep writing down your thoughts and do not stop exploring and investigating till all the thoughts have been investigated minutely. Getting rid of your preconceived notions will help you reach new decisions, better decisions for your brighter future.

6
Watching The Movie Of Life

Look carefully at the Ayodhya within you. Ayodhya refers to the absence of *Yudh*, conflict and war; it is the state of unbroken peace within you. Consider which part of your mind needs to be cleansed. Have this confidence that Lanka – the discord in life – can be won while being seated in Ayodhya – the state of inner peace.

Everyone wants to celebrate life, but are they really worthy? If they do become worthy, then how would these festivals be celebrated? Everyone is enjoying a bit of its taste. How much more can be done with it, though? There are so many possibilities, yet man is happy with little. Man should continue to work on raising his eligibility continuously.

Comforts are man's source of happiness, but he is unaware of something that might exist beyond these comforts. If man were to know his true calling, then he would insist on working on it during his lifetime; otherwise there are several ways of delaying it. He can delay it till the last breath of his life. Even at his deathbed, if he is reminded of his true calling, he could say, "Let me first complete writing my will. Several things have been left unmentioned and need to be rewritten."

When man embarks on a journey, he needs to have the eligibility or competence for it. His eligibility is being prepared from the beginning through various situations that are handcrafted by nature in his life. However, he frequently tends to forget and starts taking things for granted; he stops working on his eligibility.

When you are worthy of something, you receive it naturally.

So how do you become eligible to celebrate life to the fullest? If you want to give it clarity, then you can give it a visual form or image, just to bring that clarity. There are several interpretations to creating this visual image, but we will talk about only one – an image that will explain who can celebrate life in the fullest sense.

The visual image would be that of Hanuman – Lord Rama's devotee, who had torn open his heart to reveal Rama and Sita within. Only that person, whose heart is truthful…where Ram is followed as the ultimate source of truth and beauty, can truly celebrate life. Therefore, Hanuman is a symbol, but this is just the partial truth. There is another part that can complete this picture, which has never been highlighted till today. What if Hanuman were to rip open his forehead or his stomach, then what would be revealed? This image is still to be decided…

Certain things can only be explained with symbolism. People were not ready to extend their imagination and understanding; hence only that part where Hanuman tears open his heart has been explained. Since you are now ready, you will receive an explanation now.

After the heart, if the head were to be opened, we would find Vibhishana there and if the stomach were to be torn open, then we would find Kumbhakarna and Ravana. This might be puzzling to people.

The Three Qualities

The human body is made up of five elements and runs on three qualities. One who understands these qualities, and utilizes them properly, rises above them. The *Panchamahabhut* or five primordial elements are earth, water, air, fire and ether. *Rajas*, *Tamas*, *Sattva* are the three qualities that operate them.

Tamas is passivity, laziness and lethargy. It is required for sleep, relaxation, or to sit in meditation. Rajas is needed for action and Sattva for equanimity and balance in making the right decisions. All three should be in the right proportion. If the proportion is disturbed even minutely, the expression of the human body-mind varies substantially.

Let's understand this with an analogy. When the three fundamental colors – red, green and blue – are combined in equal proportion, they turn into white. But if their proportion is altered even slightly, then the resultant will be far from white.

You watch colored pictures on your TV set, but they appear in the right colors only when the combination of all these three fundamental colors is in the right proportion. If any of these is not in the correct ratio, you will try to adjust it or call for a technician to repair the TV set. You would say that the picture is not the same as the 'original'.

Similarly, the combination of the three qualities that operate our body-mind should be in the right proportion. We never realize how disturbed this proportion could be and how far away from the 'original' we could be. We could make the mistake of assuming that nothing is wrong with us.

So, the right ratio of Rajas, Sattva and Tamas is needed. Tamas is needed for relaxing. When you need to meditate, you need to sit calmly and concentrate. If Rajas is higher in proportion, it will prevent you from sitting calmly for a longer stretch of time. You will be restless, because your brain will be preoccupied, thinking about all the other pending jobs that are there.

When you look at people, you can immediately figure out the predominant quality in them. It is the one that defines the individual's personality. These qualities direct your life story.

If Hanuman tears open his head, then Vibhishana will be revealed. Vibhishana represents the Sattva. The quality of Sattva brings piety, equanimity and balance in life. Ravana represents Rajas, which drives one to fulfil ambitions and chase after desires. Now you would have figured out what Kumbhakarna represents. The one who sleeps for months represents the quality of Tamas – lethargy.

What kind of kingdom do you have? The kingdom here does not mean a physical place. It refers to your body-mind. Ayodhya is the sacred place where there is no conflict; it means your heart. How is your Lanka? Where do Ravana, Kumbhakarna and Vibhishana reside within you? If their positions were interchanged, if the order of their positions gets disrupted, there would be complete chaos in your life.

The order of these qualities in Hanuman is the best. Because the qualities were in the perfect order and correct ratio, it resulted in happiness, devotion, service and remembrance of Lord Rama. As soon as the order is broken, it results in chaos.

How do we remember Kumbhakarna today? Is he revered or abhorred? Who do you fondly remember? Is it Krishna? How are Meera, Radha or Draupadi remembered? Each character reminds you of a particular trait and tells you something about what was predominant in their lives. So, Hanuman sets a good example and tells us of the correct order. It is important that you open up your head to reveal the quality of Sattva. It is well known that in Ramayana, Vibhishana was appointed the Prime Minister of Lanka.

Directing The Three Qualities

How would be the kingdom that is ruled by Sattva? Hanuman revealed that Lord Ram resided in his heart; so that there would not be any mismanagement, since all the three qualities have been directed correctly from the heart.

If the directions are correct, then Rajas will also benefit you; you would want to do a lot of things. Alexander decided to conquer the entire world. It was Rajas which drove him to. Rajas bubbles like the lava within us. Alexander was unable to direct it properly. Had he known how to do that, imagine what wonders he could have brought upon this world!

So, what is inside Hanuman's stomach? Ravana and Kumbhakarna. He has swallowed them.

When Hanuman was going to Lanka, intent on finding Sita, Mount Mainak had invited him to rest. What does this indicate? Mount Mainak is symbolic of Tamas. To pause a while and rest. But Hanuman's reply was, "Not yet! I am going on Lord Rama's mission, and I need to complete it first before I stop." This shows the way Rajas was well directed in Hanuman. It got directed well because Ram was in his heart. Important work gets done first and the rest naturally falls in place.

Right Contemplation

Hanuman's appearance can be deceptive. Instead, take a look inside his heart, head and stomach. What resides over there? Similarly do not go by your own external appearances, look within yourself. If what is within you is in the correct order, then you are the most beautiful person in the whole world.

You would then be happy and create happiness for those around you, because all the three qualities are moving in the right order and direction. To celebrate life, you need to put all the three qualities in the right proportion. If this is clear, then you can celebrate life.

You can identify when these three qualities are active in your life and you need to contemplate on how to use them to your advantage. With the right understanding comes the flow of Ganga or knowledge.

Let The Ganga Flow Successfully

How have the images been depicted? Ganga flows from Shiva's hairlocks, Hanuman tears open his heart to reveal Rama and Sita's images! How are these possible? All these are reflections.

You may not be aware, but as you hear this, the knowledge or Ganga is flowing! Just as it is flowing now, it should flow at all times – in the marketplace, at the workplace, at home. If you learn this art, then you are successful.

You might question that when you cannot see the knowledge or Ganga flowing, then how can it happen. Knowledge flows continuously, irrespective of its visibility. Ganga flows. This Ganga, this contemplation that you do is completely dependent on your input.

It means that as the input, so is the output. Just like the juice that comes when you put sugarcane into the juicer. But what will happen instead, if you were to put in hay?

Be Aware Of What Is Going Inside the Ganga

Whatever you are seeing, hearing or thinking is entering your system. What are your sensory receptors perceiving? If you are aware and conscious, you will see the in-flow of pure Ganga. You will achieve a state of infinite happiness, which in turn touches everyone around you with its glow.

What you are looking at makes all the difference; everything depends on where your attention goes. Are you looking at the two people or the space between those two people? One who fills himself with hate for others, is actually filling himself with disease. The Ganga is flowing; it is just that he is not aware of the dirt and filth in it. What leaks out when you empty an abscess? It releases more disease. Ganga is flowing, but it is filthy because of the thoughts that man entertains.

You go to a theatre to see a colorful movie; how do you watch it? Just imagine, that the audience in the theatre is all Shiva. Every person in the theatre is Shiva. The movie is playing and each Shiva has his own Ganga flowing, according to what he is watching. This is how it is; the flow of Ganga is dependent on what is being watched.

The way you watch a film at the theatre decides how the knowledge flows. What are you focusing on when you watch a scene? Is it the main actors, the side actors, or the chorus in the background? Or are you concentrating on the space in between all this chaos and humdrum? Or do you try to figure out the camera position, while capturing the scene? A new perspective needs to be adopted.

We can bring about changes in the way we view things. We need to raise our awareness as to what is flowing in our lives – is it the knowledge that Ganga represents? Or is our petty desires that represent ignorance?

We need to raise our conscious awareness of who we truly are! If we are Shiva, then what should flow? Is Shiva forgetting Himself? Which quality is predominantly occupying Shiva's attention – Rajas, Tamas or Sattva? Ganga should flow in its purest form.

Achieving The Ability To See The Formless

We are able to see all things around us that have definite forms, but how do we see the formless, that which is obvious and yet invisible? We see people and their actions around us, but what are we really observing? The visible or the invisible? Where is our focus?

The story goes that Shiva kept Ravana under His feet for thousands of years. Ravana found that there was *Kailashpati* and Kailash, two things that were bigger than his Lanka; so he wanted to conquer them.

He was filled with Rajas and was under the misconception that he was the biggest and strongest in the entire world, just like Alexander, who wanted to win over the world. Curious to know who is Kailashpati, Ravana was willing to bring Mount Kailash to Lanka. The same habit of overpowering everything and possessing everything as his own, made him kidnap Sita as well.

Rajas constantly puts you on the move; planning and plotting till the end. Likewise, Ravana also planned to bring Mount Kailash to Lanka. Because this quality makes the person an over-achiever, he is constantly plans big projects, even believes that he can win the world. But if Rajas is directionless, it is wasted. If it is properly directed, it can bring great happiness to people.

However, since Ravana's Rajas was directionless, it led to him to pick up Mount Kailash and as a consequence, he was trampled under Shiva's feet for thousands of years. This is how the story narrates his life. Ravana went into a meditative state for so many years, not because of his wisdom, but because he was trampled by Shiva. It is important to develop the right understanding for meditation.

Meditate With Right Understanding

People practice meditation in many ways. Then they say, "I experienced this unique thing today; I felt some different vibrations today!" But all that does not bring about any change in their understanding. That is why we need to lay such a lot of emphasis on gaining the right understanding.

By listening to such bizarre accounts, those who meditate ask questions about why certain fancy things do not happen to them during their meditation. They are very curious about the entire process – what happens before, during and after meditation? But the emphasis should be on what you learn in the process. What conviction you achieve from meditation. Did it raise your understanding about life in any way?

Meditation done for a shorter duration but with the right understanding is more effective and beneficial. Otherwise, despite having several years of experience, Ravana was not able to achieve anything, because his intentions were wrong. When he emerged from his meditative state, he realized that he was worthless compared to Shiva. He became a devotee of Shiva. But despite rigorous penance, due to his predominant Rajas, Ravana lacked understanding and was unable to utilize Shiva's blessings properly.

To appease Shiva, Ravana cut off his heads one by one. Shiva did not change His mind until finally, Ravana was about to cut his last, tenth head. He kept cutting off his heads because he had many. He felt, "I have so many heads. Giving away some of them will not make much difference!" When offerings are made in this manner, just because it is an extra possession, then it does not appease God.

Hence, Shiva was not appeased till Ravana decided to cut off the last head that was full of pride, the head that represents the ego. This is the most important symbol in this story. Ravana kept giving with the thought, "I am giving my head." Till the time the 'I' and 'my' are based on a notion of being separate, God is not pleased.

When there was no separate 'my' (head) left, Ravana offered his own (I) head and then Shiva appeared. The story carries such a beautiful message. Till the time the ego exists, you cannot be free. It is only when you let go of the 'I' that God descends upon you.

Cycle Of Life And Death

Shiva appeared only when Ravana offered his last head. However, Ravana wished that Shiva should enter the biggest Shivaling. Ravana wanted to take that Shivaling home to Lanka. He could have asked for anything, but Ravana ultimately wanted something for himself – that he should be able to take the Shivaling back home with him!

This is the seemingly endless cycle of life and death; people remain stuck in their desires. Ravana did not find salvation despite having conducted arduous meditation, having visited Kailash and being graced by Shiva. Man is trapped by his desire to gain power, to command respect and fame through his experiences of meditation.

Ravana was stuck in Rajas, was not balanced. Tamas and Rajas – Kumbhakarna and Ravana – were not balanced. Sattva was not given its due importance; Vibhishana was not considered of any importance. He was always giving the right advice. He repeatedly advised, "Return Sita," but his words went unheeded.

The reward that Ravana asked from Shiva for his deep penance, was that Shiva should enter the biggest Shivaling, which he could carry home. He wanted to keep Shiva, the almighty, the all-powerful, by his side; so that he could enslave the entire world with Shiva by his side.

Shiva is the source of the holy trinity – Brahma-Vishnu-Mahesh. Ravana wanted to become all-powerful himself; hence he wanted Shiva – the biggest and most powerful of all the Gods by his side. So this one desire of Ravana proved fatal for him. However far a person may go in life, however much he may achieve, one single desire can stop him from attaining salvation.

He has to go even beyond Sattva as that too is not the final thing. Rajas and Tamas require more work to be done. Laziness is not a good asset and Rajas will not allow him to sit peacefully. It will force him to restlessly work, driven by ambitions. Therefore, work needs to be done on both these aspects. He will be eternally searching for something. Hence, Rajas needs to be given the right direction.

So, appointing Vibhishana or Sattva as the Prime Minister and Rajas as the army-chief is sensible. All-powerful, Rajas has to be put in commanding position of the army, under the directions of Sattva – the Prime Minister. Tamas has to be imprisoned, while the King becomes an unparalleled supreme being, rising above the three qualities (*gunas*).

A kingdom with such values and such an arrangement will be a perfect role model for others. Just like Ayodhya, a perfect kingdom with no flaws. Can you close your eyes and think about *Ram-rajya* – the rule by Lord Rama? How was it? Think about it carefully.

Cloak yourself differently and make a round of your kingdom – your body-mind – to verify if it is still the perfect one like Ram-rajya. Or does it have any flaws, any cause for unhappiness? Close your eyes and do a mental verification whether there are any ill-effects of Lanka in the kingdom of your life.

Ravana prayed and requested Shiva to sit in the Shivaling and took him along to the city of gold, Lanka. He downgraded Mount Kailash to an inhabitable place and suggested that his city of gold was a better abode for Shiva. Imagine his audacity to actually insist on taking Shiva to Lanka!

Shiva Needs To Be Awakened

Despite the close proximity to God, there is still the need to wake up Shiva. Maha Shivaratri symbolizes that. You visit temples to celebrate Maha Shivaratri.

The Rudra dance happens when Shiva is enraged, while the Tandav is done when Shiva is pleased. Maha Shivaratri comes as an occasion to check with the Shiva within you – how is He finding it?

Visiting temples provides a perfect foil to break the monotony of routine life. With routine mechanical living, one follows the old thinking process. At the temple, people expect a different atmosphere. They feel that here they are in a better frame of mind to question the God within – question whether is He appeased or upset.

But the one who has truly understood, can ask Shiva anytime, anywhere, whether He is pleased with him. "Stay pleased always, continue doing your Tandav dance!" will be his sincere prayer.

Watching The Satarang Movie

If you have learned this knack of seeing Shiva wherever you look, then you are eligible to celebrate life. For this, you need to learn to watch the '*Satarang*' movie in the right manner.

What is Shiva? He is the source of '*tarang*' or vibration. He is an amalgamation of Brahma, Vishnu, Mahesh. He is the source of Rajas, Tamas and Sattva.

Today, science accepts that the world is a cosmic orchestra of vibrations. The vibrations are of different frequencies. When the speed is fast, objects appear solid. It's their varying frequencies that create man, animal and stone. All the three have the same vibration at the core – the dance of Shiva. Because of the difference in the speed of vibrations, we get different kinds of matter – solid, liquid or gas. Whether ice, water or steam, the element remains the same.

All of this is just an expression – Shiva's ongoing dance!

If we cannot see it, we get bored after some time. It is the same routine of life with the same tasks, and the same monotonous lifestyle. But if we do not understand the deep reason behind this game of life, then we won't be able to appreciate the cosmic movie – the Satarang movie.

Imagine an auditorium, where there are many Shivas seated, watching the Satarang movie. You must understand the meaning of the word, 'Satarang'. 'Sa' is Sattva, 'Ta' is Tamas, 'Ra' is Rajas, and then 'Ga' stands for *Gunateet*. The moment you understand, it will be your 'Eureka' moment! The day you understand how to watch the 'Satrang' (or colorful) movie in the right manner will be the day that you realize your true happiness.

God – The Creator, Coordinator And Director

With the story of Shiva, we understand that vibrations surround us at all times. It is the dance that we see all around us. Brahma, Vishnu and Mahesh are the creator, coordinator and director.

Brahma is the creator of all. Vishnu is playing the role of the coordinator so that the film is not playing in any random order. Shiva is given the role of the audience. He watches the movie and will raise His hands with thumbs-down whenever He wants the movie to end. Shiva has used several hand gestures, but none to stop the movie. But He could gesture the end of the movie when He is fed up!

If there are no Self-realized souls remaining on Earth, then He will be fed up. He would say, "There is no one, who can watch the movie as I would like to watch it." But as there are still many who are available to watch the movie of this world from that pure standpoint, there is no question of the world coming to an end.

People are scared that the world will come to an end. When will that happen? When Shiva, the audience, decides that He has had enough and does not want to watch anymore. Hands raised, thumbs facing down – the sign for "Done! Done with it!"

So, Shiva has been given the role of ending the movie when He wants to. The others' task is to keep the film rolling. Shiva is enjoying Himself thoroughly so far. But there is a possibility that He might forget the importance of His role. Just as a general audience would at some point, He might give the thumbs-down sign of DISLIKE or STOP. In order to make sure that Shiva does not forget the importance of His role, the Guru was introduced with the role of reminding Him!

So, now you might understand the meaning of the couplet, "*Gurur Brahma…Gurur Vishnu… Gurur Devo Maheshwara*" Why was the Guru given such an important role? This arrangement was made to keep a check on Shiva. Otherwise there was the danger that He might get bored and decide to end the film even before the interval. We have not even reached the interval as yet.

All this is symbolic. The Guru and Shiva are both aspects of the same Supreme Being. The Guru is an aspect that directs towards the Truth. Shiva has also been called *Adi Guru*. The Guru has the role of reminding Bholenath, who is prone to forget His responsibility as the audience. It becomes a necessity to personify these aspects of the One Being separately, only to explain what is going on.

Shiva might raise His hand and indicate the feared Stop sign. But the Guru will convince Him to keep His hands down, "Hands down… hands down!" Shiva will continue watching and enjoying the film. He is learning the knack of watching the movie and enjoying it.

And as soon as He starts to get a little bored and raise His hands, the Guru immediately wakes Him up, "O my Dear Shiva… Wake up.. Look around You… What are You doing! Ask Yourself, 'Who am I now?' Earlier You were a bored person, a person who was fed up, but who are You now?"

The Director's Point Of View

The Guru will question Shiva, "Were You lost in the characters of the movie? Look in between those characters; look behind those characters; see who is operating all this; look at the scene behind, look at the cameraman and the position of the cameras while filming the movie.

"Focus on who is giving the input to the cameraman. What is the Director doing? Look and try to understand what is going on in the Director's mind. Consider His point of view. What instructions did He give to the cameraman? What is the Director trying to highlight in the film? The actor, or the actress, or something else? Why did He make such an arrangement?"

If all this is understood, then Shiva's Tandav dance will continue in the theatre of life. Wake up Shiva…wake up!

So then, how is your presence in the theatre of life now? How much are you enjoying the 'Satarang' movie? Are you just happy or do you even want to dance? Your response will be according to whatever your condition is right now.

Everyone is watching the movie of their own life and their reason for dancing will be according to that. You do not dance just because you want to imitate others while they are dancing. Everyone has to honestly look within at their own internal state to understand the presence of Shiva within themselves.

The 'Satarang' movie continues and it is up to Shiva to indicate how long to continue the movie; when to show appreciation or express wonder. But how does He indicate that the film will continue? Shiva's Tandav is the thumbs-up that He gives to show that He is loving it! Through His Tandav dance, He indicates that the film shall continue, for many more weeks, many more years, and many more ages to come!

There will be many events and incidents in your lives where you will need to apply this knowledge. You may see something in the movie of your life that upsets you. And yet, if you see it from the Director's standpoint, you will put your thumbs up and laugh, "Continue…Continue."

Real application of this understanding happens when you are dealing with situations at home, in the marketplace, at the workplace. Outside the house, you will have to control the expression of your happiness. How can you sing loudly and dance enthusiastically there?

But there are some places where it is possible to dance. It is this that man forgets many times. He sits at home but forgets to dance. This is one place where he can let go of all his inhibitions. Dancing here is symbolic of enjoying the movie of Life and expressing wonder at its beauty. Due to inhibitions, one is neither able to sing praises nor express wonder, nor even look at oneself objectively. If man were to remember this, life would abound in bliss despite its challenges.

Contemplate on the various incidents of your life so far. How do you see them now? There may have been situations where you felt like putting your thumbs-down, being fed up of the movie. But are you now able to happily say "Continue"? Are you convinced about the real purpose – the Director's point of view – behind those life scenes?

This is why, it is important to develop the habit of contemplation. With well-directed contemplation, the Ganga of knowledge will flow. Positive and happy thoughts contribute to purification of the Ganga – the flow of knowledge.

How can it be dirty if your intentions are pure! If you understand this, then you will always make efforts to keep the flow of Ganga pure and fresh in your life. The elixir of life will flow endlessly and you will witness the bliss. Life will then be a celebration.

Watch the 'Satarang' movie playing in your mind, in your body. What are the vibrations that you can witness? Pleasure, wonder, joy, peace, love, devotion… are you witnessing every state? If you watch it like Shiva, life will be like the Tandav dance of Nataraja, purifying the Ganga within you, bringing you bliss.

There are numerous topics that we think about in life. But do they give such bliss, such wonder, such delight!? Contemplation on Shiva leads to endless bliss… unconditional bliss that can be enjoyed every moment of life!

One human body can fall short of being able to handle such a flow of bliss. One body is not enough to celebrate it, to soak in the bliss! Hence the Ganga of this knowledge will naturally overflow from within you and touch everybody, spreading the bliss!

You need to be able to watch the 'Satarang' film from Shiva's standpoint to truly celebrate Maha Shivaratri. The divine orchestra of vibrations everywhere! How should you watch it, to make sure that the Ganga that flows is pious and pure?

We have seen the play of Rajas, Tamas and Sattva within us. If we are *Tamasic*, then we will find excuses and the comforts of life that pull us towards them. Any kind of interruption to comfort will cause irritation. If Tamas has become predominant, it needs to be worked upon. Shiva needs to be awakened; the *Gunateet* state, which is beyond the three *gunas*, needs to be awakened to balance the gunas.

It is difficult to have mental stillness when Rajas is predominant. It is impossible to sit in silent meditation as thoughts of activity and fulfilment of desires play havoc. Chasing after desires becomes the main priority.

Tamas and Rajas – the Kumbhakarna and Ravana within us – need to be swallowed and placed in the stomach, so that they do not dominate.

Sattva should be in the head – balanced and pious. The Gunateet state – the state of Shiva – should reign from the heart. Rajas should be given the role of the commander-in-chief to execute actions. The excess Tamas should be put in prison.

Sattva will be the minister to manage affairs and the Gunateet state will preside as the king. If you work upon your body-mind in this way, you will be able to celebrate life in the kingdom of your body.

Understanding the true meaning of these symbols without getting stuck in them will be your greatest blessing. This is how you can truly practice Shiv Sadhana – the practice of alignment with Shiva. What was invisible thus far will become visible. But if you again get entangled in your comfort zone, in worldly desires and ambitions, your progress towards your life purpose will be nullified. All your efforts would be wasted.

The Satarang movie is the play of SA – Sattva, TA – Tamas, RA – Rajas, G – Gunateet. When you are out in the world, remind yourself that the Satarang movie is being played – not just outside, but also within your mind. What will Shiva within you say – Continue or Stop? Listen to your Shiva. If Shiva is asleep, then recall the Guru for right guidance.

The ego, the "I, Me, Mine" has to be surrendered to God. You have to make your own system for constantly reminding yourself. It is only when devotion within you is uncompromising that you will want to do something, to change something.

Applying this art of watching the movie of life is of vital importance in daily life. The point is to keep reminding yourself, because if one forgets, then the entire exercise of creating this drama is wasted. Without remembering the real purpose, man would live a mechanical existence, just like any other animal. You may see others around you choosing to live differently. But what is your choice?

Nature has designed human life so that it continues through further generations. The idea is to maintain the existence of human life. But Shiva's Shivani – Mother Nature – needs to be shown the path. If Shiva is awake, the path will be shown automatically.

The picture of *Ardhnarishwar* shows how Shivani is in perfect alignment with Shiva. But Shivani can fall out of alignment if Shiva is asleep. We need to wake up the Shiva within us.

You are being given so many examples, so that when time comes, you will remember at least some of them. Something will wake you up and make you question your actions.

Are you pointing your thumbs down or up? Can you find something worth wondering and praising even in a testing situation or are you going to be bitter about it? What are you actually doing when you complain and resist what is going on in the world? You are pointing your thumbs down to indicate that such a world is not worth living in.

If you truly understand the whole picture of what is going on, then you can become an example for others. You need to gain understanding of the essence of Shiva to make sure that Shiva does not point the thumbs down due to lack of awareness, to ensure that he continues his graceful, happy, and blessed dance. If you understand, you will automatically want to ensure this. Nobody will have to force you to attend discourses, because you would have gained the capacity to look within yourself and understand your role in the cosmic scheme.

The audience of the film is Shiva. And the audience's votes is of vital importance to the continuation of the movie of life. All reality shows are dependent on the audience's votes; not just on TV, but also in the reality show of this world. Even the judges' decisions go unheard! In the finals, it is just the audience's votes that makes a difference. This means that if the audience or public were to become negative, it would spell out the end of show, otherwise it would carry on.

The role of the Guru is to ensure that Shiva does not forget His true nature. The Shiva within you should be awakened, so that the dance of life can continue in happiness. The Shiva within you is the audience of this movie of your life. If more than 50% of the beings in the world start pointing their thumbs down, then it would signal the end of this cosmic show.

Awareness needs to be brought to the masses. If masses are awakened, then they would want to raise the awareness of others around them. Otherwise what kind of feedback will they give? If people are bogged down by thinking about superficial things like potholes on the roads and corruption, then when will they think about the real problem. When will they focus on raising mass consciousness, which will automatically solve the real problems in their lives!

If people's consciousness is at a high level, they will automatically want to share this perspective. They will want to make this film more beautiful and will praise it even more. The more people appreciate the inherent beauty of this creation and praise the creator, the faster the automatic solving happens.

Everyone will find their inner peace, which in turn will eventually result in World peace, because everyone is content within themselves. How easy it seems, but we have to understand, experience and remember it for the future.

At what times do we forget and where all do we focus on negatives? If you entertain negative thoughts about someone, then you are throwing dirt into the Ganga. Check the water of Ganga; if it is pure, then Shiva is pleased that Ganga is getting pure after being dirty for so long.

It's like opening a tap which was closed for many years. The water that flows out initially is going to be dirty and muddy. But if you let the water flow for some time continuously, eventually the water starts becoming cleaner.

So is the case with the water of life. It has to be made a priority. Man has a habit of procrastinating things; he doesn't want to change. He is unable to stop himself. Ravana's ego always shows up within man.

Man is unaware of his true identity and that is why he is unable to seize the initiative. When you know your true self, you won't sacrifice the purpose of your earthly life.

The Guru within you should remind you, "Are you going to put your purpose on this earth at stake, that too on the basis of the other person's behavior towards you? What has happened to you, Shiva? How naïve are you and how soon you forget things!"

You have to make a system of reminders of the truth for yourself, so that you can raise your awareness. Put up reminders to keep you aware all the time. Love for Shiva will compel you to do this. It's the power of love! Its beauty makes you remember your loved ones. Love serves as an incredible reminder for constantly remembering whom we love.

As you acquire more knowledge, there's the danger of forgetting the truth. You would know Yudhishtira from the Mahabharata. Despite being learned and *sattvic*, he too committed the same mistake of forgetting the truth. When you forget the truth, you can put everything at stake, just as Yudhishtira did in the gambling game. There's a chance that you too might get entangled, even if you are sattvic.

When man gets attached to the label of being 'learned' or 'virtuous', he tends to forget the purpose of going beyond Sattva and finds an excuse to err. He begins to feel superior and believes he's better than others. With a bloated ego, he creates obstacles for his own progress.

With Sattva, nothing seems to hurt anymore. Earlier, when man was tamasic, it would hurt. With Rajas again, things bothered him. With Sattva, nothing seems to matter anymore. However, the Sattvic one needs to practice control over what he speaks. In speaking the truth, he sometimes forgets that truth can sometimes sound very harsh and bitter. He needs to understand that and bring compassion and empathy in his speech. Otherwise, Sattva begins to degrade due to the "I am pious; I know it all" attitude. Several Sattvic people get corrupted and lose their way in the journey of the Truth. Many even slide back to Rajasic or Tamasic ways.

When Ravana had decided to go to India, his brother Vibhishana had dissuaded him, saying that the trip would be futile. When Alexander had set out to conquer the world, his teacher, Aristotle had told him, "Where are you going? Everything is already available in Greece. Why do you go searching somewhere outside for what is already here?" Rajas does not allow man to sit idle; it constantly compels you to move from one place to another, from one activity to another. Such people travel all over the world.

Some dream of going on a world tour and they sacrifice everything else in saving money all their lives to fulfil this dream. They work endlessly and tirelessly, to save money all their lives, just to tour the world. They never realize that the world tour is of no use. You might see the whole world, but if you are unable to look within and know your true self, then what is the point!

You can do a world tour, while sitting at one place. Man does not know this because he is helpless under the influence of Rajas. It does not allow him to rest. Rajas makes the decision and convinces you to keep yourself busy with activities. Tamas, on the other hand, forces you to relax in your comfort zone.

Man feels he's in control. But it is Tamas and Rajas that are actually governing his decisions. Let Sattva make the decision in consultation with the Gunateet state. With such equipoise, the kingdom of your life will turn out to be the best.

How deep this is! We need to contemplate on these truths and remember to apply them in our lives. We need to remind ourselves as soon as any complaint arises in our heads and ask the Shiva in our heart – "Why are You gesturing the thumbs down, instead raise Your thumbs up? Continue the show!"

If someone is going around with his face puffed up in anger then remember Hanuman's face, which was always puffed up, and then enjoy the thought. Think of the angry person as Hanuman and smile to yourself thinking that the person is putting on an act of being angry so well.

He is complaining about everything and indicating with thumbs down that he is bored. He wants to stop the movie. Instead tell him, "Continue the film, Shiva!" It might seem that there's nothing worthwhile to continue, but there always is something that can become the reason for continuation.

There might be thousands of negative things in this world, but find that one thing that can become the reason to continue. Once you understand how to see the movie and continue with this perspective, imagine your state of mind when you come out of the office, out of home? You will be in a state of constant and unconditional happiness.

Otherwise, people consider others as hungry or angry; no one seems happy, neither the guest nor the host, neither the boss nor the subordinate. People are gesturing with their thumbs down. Thankfully, not everyone is like this; otherwise, the movie would have ended long time back!

If every Shiva did this, and every vibration was negative, then more than 50% people would indicate "The End" with their thumbs down. If that happens, the film is finished! In order to maintain less than 50% and prevent the votes from going up, we have to make sure that Shiva stays in an 'aware' mode at least within us.

There are some strong people who are aware of this. But the votes of those, who keep oscillating between the negative and positive, cannot be considered valid. Their votes keep changing sides.

Continuity to this movie of life comes because of those people, who are firm in their conviction and cast their votes only for "Continuation", regardless of whether the scene appears bright or bleak. The world runs on their votes. Firmness comes with knowledge, continuity comes with devotion, and this is how the cycle of life goes on.

So the Ganga of love, bliss and peace should flow. When there is an interruption to this flow, know that it is time to learn something more about life. Obstacles in life come because of the ego. The ego resists the flow of life, thus causing obstacles. Ravana's head, which was not surrendered to God, is the real obstacle. There is great happiness in removing these tiny pebbles that block this flow. Surrendering your ego to this flow brings far greater happiness than any other pleasure that the ego can desire.

Most of the time, man is not convinced about these truths and is adamant, "I do not believe all this. These are all bookish things and not real." He will refuse to tread further and will keep looking at one thing or the other, waiting for clarity to come. But clarity does not come with an adamant attitude. He does not take a step forward and does not realize what he is losing. The Guru tries to convince him, but he applies his own adamant force against the divine force. Such people keep waiting for some kind of proof to accept the truth.

We have to move on from Tamas to Rajas, from Rajas to Sattva, and from Sattva to the Gunateet state. The Gunateet state, the *Turyaateet* state – the state beyond the fourth, the *Arkaateet* state, which is beyond the realms of heaven and hell.

The Arkaateet state is the seventh level of consciousness. Wherever we are, we should aim for the seventh level, towards bringing about Maha Nirvana. We should not stop on the way at any cost.

Man is satisfied with the heaven of comforts, conveniences, and sensory pleasures. He falls into the trap of liking things and decides to stay in this comfort zone. He then decides that he need not progress any further. Do not stop in the middle. Whatever the distractions and attractions, do not stop. Once we have all the luxuries and pleasures of life, we tend to stop looking for the real truth and liberation.

Therefore, ask yourselves in all honesty, question your ability to withstand temptations realistically and sincerely. Asking the right questions sincerely will always lead to honest answers and will definitely result in progress towards your life purpose.

■

7
Transcending Duality

Throw out all your tenants who have decided to stay on long term in your house! You gave them a house for temporary residence, but if they decide to stay forever, then it is a mistake that needs to be resolved.

When was the mistake made, how was it made, and who are these tenants?

You are living in a house, where all the doors and windows are open, allowing the cool breeze to pass through. You see that people enter the house from one door and pass out from another. Later on, you see people who had been tenants, pass through the doors with their pets, like dogs, cats, pigeons, and other animals.

You are unaware about where these animals came from. But you suspect that they must have come along with the tenants. Just like the birds fly away, you believe that the tenants would also leave the house, but you do not realize that these very people soon become the reason for your headache. This is because you are not aware of what's happening behind the scene.

Sitting In Space

You are being shown what happens when you are meditating or contemplating deeply.

You are sitting in space over the clouds. Your body-mind is the house. Sitting in space is like sitting in a hall and a pigeon would fly inside and then fly out. How will you look at it? Something that keeps coming and going by itself.

You can think of it as one thought passing by, through your awareness. A thought comes, and then it goes. How does it matter to you! But the problem arises when a thought decides to stay put like a long-term tenant. It finds the atmosphere conducive for long term stay. But along with it comes its baggage of dogs, cats or pigeons. Who are these pets? Emotions are the pets that accompany thoughts.

Till the time you are unaware of their future activities, you will be undecided as to which door or window should be left open or should be closed. Where is the grill-work needed or the wire-mesh put up? From where does this thought enter? From the Internet? If one of the windows or webpage is left open, thoughts start pouring in. You need to become aware of these unwanted entries and need to take proactive steps to prevent their arrival in your mind.

What if the thoughts start claiming that they have stayed in your mind for eleven years and it is now legal for them to stay permanently? If they start showing you the legal angle, then what will you do? This is what we need to explore.

Seer, Seen And Seeing

How do you witness what is being seen, so that the "seer", the "seen" and "seeing", all unite to become one? When we use the word "seer", what we mean is the "knower", the one who is "knowing" everything that is being "known". Seer or knower – the subject, seen or known – the object, and seeing or knowing – the act... all combine into one. It is when you learn the art of seeing these three as one that you will be free from this game.

Of these three, whom do we actually consider the subject? We usually consider the mind to be the subject. The mind assumes itself to be the subject and witnesses thoughts. Things come and go, and in between, the knowing of these things happens. But, who is knowing the subject, object and action of knowing? And why?

Who is knowing or witnessing these three and what is the purpose behind witnessing? The purpose is to unite the three and know 'Oneself'.

It is just like bread slices in a sandwich. There is one slice and then tomato or cucumber in the middle and then the second slice. You combine them and press them together to make a sandwich. Likewise, you combine the seer, the scene and the seeing all together. But be careful that you do not suppress them! The idea is to press them together, but not suppress them. Suppressing happens when you get overtly involved in thoughts and feelings. Press them together with detachment and the right understanding.

The Absent-minded Mind

In the absence of understanding, the mind starts assuming itself as the subject. It thinks of itself as the seer. When the mind stands tall and separate by assuming the seer's role for itself, it cannot unite with the "seen" and "seeing". It is incapable of combining with the other two. If the mind is considered the subject, then the three cannot be combined as one, because the mind can be absentminded; it will keep looking, but it will miss seeing what is always present.

However, the real subject is always aware, for it is "awareness" itself. The real knower is always present, for it is "presence" itself! Even in deep sleep, the real subject is available, consciousness is available. And there was a time when the subject was all alone.

When Does Maha Shivaratri Come

Before Maha Shivaratri, the subject was already present, but there was nothing to be known. The seer was there, but there was nothing to be seen. When this is said, people imagine that the night was deep, allowing no light to penetrate, with no stars and no moon. There was nothing to see; so it could not have been daytime as there was no sun. So, it was named the night – Maha Shivaratri.

Shivaratri was already going on eternally, and one day came Maha Shivaratri. Maha Shivaratri comes when you want to know the state that is beyond 'two', the state beyond duality. Beyond sadness-happiness comes pure happiness; beyond silence-noise comes pure silence, beyond love and hatred comes pure love, beyond night-day comes Maha Shivaratri!

We must understand the need of creating noise to attain this pure silence. If you are standing on the riverbank and you need to cross over to the other side, will you not need a stepping-stone with the aid of which you can cross over to the other side? Likewise, to attain the state of pure silence, we need to create the stepping-stone of noise; you move from silence to noise, only to eventually transcend to pure silence. Noise was created so that we rise beyond both – silence and noise – to reach that pure silence which transcends both.

"God created this world and the chaos in it. Now we have to live in it." This very thought has become a permanent tenant in our mind. What does man think? He thinks that God created this world, this tumultuous life, and that man has to bear everything, bear all the pain and problems. Unfortunately, man is unable to grasp the higher perspective beyond this. This is the limitation of thoughts!

What was the primary purpose behind making the world like this? Does man have to stop because of the problems he faces? Stopping indicates no movement; it means stagnation, and hence there is no growth. Stopping in the journey is not an option. If the journey continues, then it achieves the real purpose of Maha Shivaratri.

Pure Silence – Beyond The Two States

Why did Maha Shivaratri come? So that it can be followed by day; then the night that comes after the day will be *Maharatri* – the big night. Without bringing in the day, you cannot bring in the night.

What will you call as *Maha*? That which goes beyond the two states, beyond opposites.

The night was already there, however, what needed to be brought in was Maha Shivaratri. One who is unable to grasp this might respond, "How crazy! Day after night, and then beyond both, a Maharatri!"

This is a profound truth. It is when you understand it that you will be able to stay in the experience of pure silence, while still living actively in the world. The word "stabilization" can be used for this. You will continue to observe the world, but you will make a sandwich of all the three – the seer, the act of seeing, and the seen.

The real knower, which is uniting all these three, is actually not a part of them, and is able to objectively witness this three-in-one. However, the real knower is actually not interest in the ingredients of this three-in-one sandwich. The real knower's interest lies in knowing oneself – the real self.

The sandwich of 'seer, scene, seeing,' serves as a reflective medium, like a mirror. Imagine this kind of sandwich in which one side of the bread slice is a mirror. When you look at the sandwich, all you can see is yourself in it! With this comes recognition of Self.

Actually, the real subject is Shiva, the real you. That means the subject is you, and the object is also you, the knowing is also you. This is something that can only be experienced by *being* it. It cannot be understood by conceptualizing or imagining it.

The Artist Is Outside

Consider a painting in which there is a man standing and watching a kite flying high in the sky. The man is the "seer", who is "seeing" the flying kite that is "seen". So, this "seer, seeing and the seen" are part of the painting. But the artist of this painting is outside!

The artist is depicting that the man is watching the kite. But, the artist is observing his own art, the picture he has painted – the way he has drawn the man and the kite. Why has he painted whatever he has painted?

The painting is the artist's way of celebrating himself, of celebrating his creativity. The painting helps the artist to understand his own self – the real 'I'. Here you can see that the three – the seer, scene and seeing – are united as one, but the actual observer, the artist, is outside the painting. It is only when he creates a work of art that he knows himself as an artist!

When you observe a scene, you are aware that your mind is watching the scene. But, there is this awareness that the mind is also being known. When the mind is assumed as the seer, the seen world comes under the mind's microscope. But, the real seer places the mind under the microscope. The mind is also being known. And the purpose of knowing the mind is not to know the details in the mind, but to know the knower of the mind; to know the knower of thoughts; to realize the real Self – Shiva.

Double-Screen Analogy

Let's understand this with the help of the example of a television. Televisions that we watch have the screen in front. But you wouldn't have seen a television that has a screen at the back too. Let us imagine such a double-screen television.

Now, the screen at the back has a torch behind it, whose light is flashing on the screen. The torch's light flashes on the back-screen, bounces off the screen and is reflected back on the torch itself, making the torch glow in its own light.

Now, what if there was no television at all? What if the torch was present all alone? You can imagine the torch flashing its light continuously, way ahead into endless space. But its light does not get a chance to be reflected as there is nothing to reflect it. The reflection of light on the source would not happen without a reflecting screen.

It is a an auspicious wish that creates something that can reflect the light back onto the torch. Why did Maha Shivaratri come? It came with this auspicious wish, that the knower be known through its own light of knowing. When the Knower is known, then the purpose of creating the mirror is served.

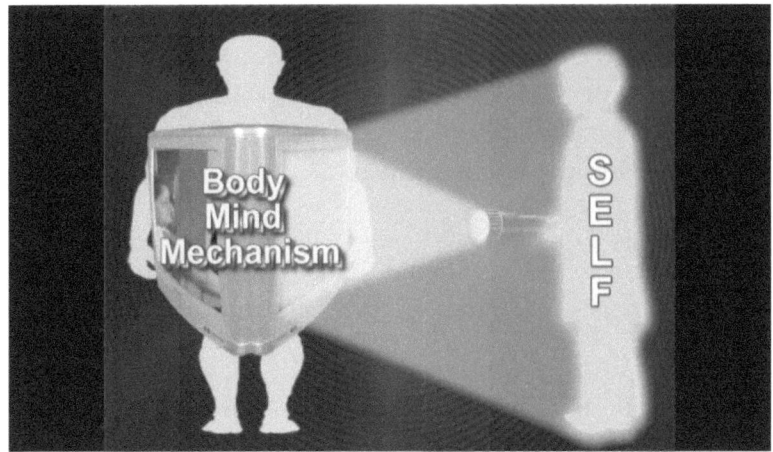

So then who is Shiva, and what is Shakti? Shiva is the Knower and Shakti is the mirror through which Shiva knows himself. Shiva gives rise to Shakti; the dancer creates the dance to know his own nature.

The double-screen television in the analogy is Shakti. It is only when the torchlight hits the back screen of the television that the light gets the opportunity to be reflected back on the torch. In experiencing the dance, the dancer is actually experiencing himself!

But is that all that is happening here? No, there is more. As soon as the torchlight falls upon the back screen, the front screen gets switched on and there are multiple channels playing.

One of the channels is playing a serial where the character is narrating his life story, of the various experiences that he has experienced in his life. He questions, "Why me? Why did all this happen to me?" This is playing on the screen.

The torch illuminates other objects, but is also getting self-illuminated. But with this comes the additional bonus – the vision of other programs, stories, illusions, other characters, the false 'I', multiple I's functioning through numerous bodies.

This television screen that plays the various channels can be predominantly Tamasic, Rajasic, or Sattvic. The television here refers to the body-mind mechanism. Predominant Tamas brings passivity with it; the characters walk slowly. It's like an Art movie! Rajas on the other hand, brings fast-paced action movies. Sattva is responsible for equanimity with its balance. So Rajas, Tamas, Sattva denote passivity, motility, and equanimity.

All these are playing out in the characters; but what should happen in these characters? One should actually go beyond these three qualities. One should transcend these attributes to the Gunateet state.

If we go beyond the three attributes, then how will the television play? How will the body-mind function? With Tamas, it will play only black-and-white pictures and with Rajas, it will play in color. But if the color TV's antenna is facing the wrong direction, the Rajas would be misdirected. So, Rajas needs direction, while Tamas needs color – action and motivation. Rajas needs to be directed correctly towards Sattva.

Alexander should have been told that instead of trying to conquer India, he should come to learn and advance his wisdom. Being directed on the correct path enables the Rajasic one to move towards Sattva.

What would a color TV that represents Sattva be like? Its brightness will be in sync with its contrast; there would be equanimity. And beyond Sattva comes the Gunateet state.

The TV here means your body-mind mechanism. So, if your body is functioning from the Gunateet state – the state beyond the three – then you are in the experience of the real Self, the real seer will be awakened.

With the Gunateet state, what kind of color TV would it be? One with an auto-correction system! The auto-correction system means that the TV setting varies according to the situation. During the day, it is a different setting, given the brightness of daytime. At night, it is different due to the lack of external light. Settings also vary based on whether the program is colored or black-and-white.

When the auto-correction mode is not active, the black-and-white programs also have some tint of color in them. The white is never pure white; there is a slightly reddish hue in it. So, without the auto-correction that comes from being in the Gunateet state, one would lead a black-and-white life, that is shaded by the redness of anger or hatred. But with the auto-correction setting switched on, apt responses will be given depending on situations.

While sitting in meditative state, the auto-correction system will use Tamas. When actions have to be performed, it will activate Rajas. Sattva will be employed to make balanced decisions. To do this, you need to be in the fourth state, the Gunateet – beyond the three gunas.

What kind of a television was functioning in Lord Krishna's life… how was the volume control working in it? In the Gunateet state, the volume is altered as per need. It detects the situation and decides whether the volume needs to be in softer and hushed or loud and rushed. What should the volume be when it is on the battlefield? And what should the volume be when a discourse is being delivered in a hall? It detects and decides according to the requirement.

The television example shows that while the television is playing and capturing attention, the real audience is Shiva – the torch, the source of light. Shiva projects light on the back screen, reflecting the light on Himself. On the front screen, films start playing, all kinds of films – tragedies, horror stories, comedies, etc. Everyone has their own different films playing.

When the real knower begins to know himself, then what kind of a film would it be? Shiva will be lit in His own light within each one of you. If Shiva is self-shining, self-aware within each one of you, then what kind of a movie will you see? This movie will express the third state – pure happiness, beyond sorrow and joy, beyond life and death, beyond chaos and peace. Such a movie can be played only when the Shiva within you awakens.

This can happen only when you start understanding your body-mind and your real Self. You need to understand the purpose behind the creation of the body-mind mechanism. The purpose of realizing the true Self and stabilizing in it.

Thoughts that arise in your awareness are just tourists; do not let them find a permanent place to stay inside. Moreover, they come with their pets and create ruckus. Pets like anger, sadness, guilt, which bring pain to you.

The presence of sadness indicates that it is time for you to close the windows of your mind. You should be aware of which window needs to be left open or be closed. If some thoughts ask for your permission to enter your house (mind), then you need to have such awareness as to politely but firmly refuse them entry.

There are already, multiple tenants that have taken permanent residence within you: "I am Indian", "I am fair", "I am dark", "I am this religion or that," etc. Along with them have come their pets as well and you believe that you are male or female, tall or short, fair or dark. These are aspects of your body-mind, not you.

You need to ask yourself, 'Who am I now? A little while earlier, maybe I was bored, or confused, or angry. But right now, who am I?' Being bored, or confused, or angry are states of the mind, the pets that come along with thoughts. Who are you?

When you ask yourself, "Who am I now?" then does your attention turn back towards its source, towards the torch of awareness that is throwing light on everything else? The film played on the screen is being seen through the senses of sight, sound, touch, taste and smell. But you go behind the screen, because the torch is outside.

The experience of your true Self, the feeling of being alive, is sensed due to the presence of the body. Hence you tend to believe that the experience of the Self is inside you. But the actual fact is, that your body and your sense of the world are inside the experience; everything is in the Self.

Seeing The Comedy Of Life

The usual comedy that people enjoy is at the expense of others, ridiculing others. People laugh at the fall of others because they see their own downfalls and feel nice that there are others too who are experiencing life like them. This comedy emerges from the head.

But the moment you finally understand the comedy of the heart, you will feel liberated. This is a comedy only when you actually understand it. Life is a joke; the question is who will tell whom? The Self is all that exists! When the real comedy starts, it will be from the heart. There is unconditional happiness in liberation.

So what kind of a comedy film will this be? For such a film to play on the screen and for you to enjoy it, you need to shift towards the torch, the source of the light, the source of knowing. It is there, that you will be in the Gunateet state beyond Tamas, Rajas and Sattva. It is the state beyond the mind where you will gain the ability to make the right decisions that will be for the wellbeing of all.

Otherwise, without this clarity, the screen always looks foggy. You would say that there is noise on the screen. Nothing is visible clearly. Decisions are taken reactively mostly as they appear on the screen.

When there is confusion, you should ask, "With whom is this happening? Is this happening with me or with the TV set?" When you question yourself in this way, you will be rid of the effect of negative thoughts. On the contrary, you will feel that a few blemishes are good, if they help in reminding you of who you truly are!

Every negative thought will serve to remind you of conducting Self-enquiry. Self-enquiry will help you to use your thoughts in the right way, by making them a mirror for yourself. You should do this with all the thoughts, but if not all, then at least those that make you sad.

Incidents, thoughts and sorrow are all intricately linked. You might think otherwise. You might even believe that an incident is directly responsible for your sorrow. What is the link between them? It's the thoughts that arises within you in between that causes sorrow.

The incident being the same, one may feel indifferent to it depending on the thoughts that arise within. Some others may feel disappointed, again depending on the kind of thoughts that they entertain in reaction to the same incident.

You must get this shift in understanding – thoughts, if allowed to become tenants in your mind, will eventually result in bringing sadness. Introspect the thoughts that come to you. The thoughts that try to become long-term tenants in your mind and cause grief should be shunned. Understand those thoughts carefully and observe which window they enter from. Then you will know which windows need to be closed permanently and which are to be left open.

The tenants that plan to stay on long term should be analyzed completely, minutely. You should question them about any accompanying pets. If the answer is in affirmative, then immediately show them the exit door!

You have to objectively analyze every lingering thought without being prejudiced. If you are able to objectively do such self-analysis without getting embroiled in thoughts, then the television will continue to play properly.

Fulfilling Shiva's Will

A child picks up a pencil for the first time and draws something on a sheet of paper. He enjoys the experience thoroughly. And then his father, who is an artist, comes and looks at the drawing. He is immediately pleased with the sketch and knows that it is invaluable. Now both the father and son are happy.

What is the difference then? The child expressed his inner joy through his drawing; but the father realizes its value.

The father can understand the child's happiness and perceive the child's innocent essence reflecting in the picture. He would wish that the child understands his perspective so that the child is motivated to draw more of such pictures in future, with the artist's perspective.

We go through a lot of experiences in our lives…we satisfy the desires of our body, mind and senses. One day, unknowingly, by chance, we fulfil Shiva's wish, the dancer's desire. Shiva is indicative of the real Self, the living essence that is present within each one of us.

But unfortunately, we are unable to identify it or grasp the importance of fulfilling Shiva's desire, though it gives us immense joy. We may say, "It was a lovely experience! I achieved personal gratification by assisting others…"

But when we grasp the value of fulfilling the Self's desire, then we would want to fulfil the Self's will consciously.

8
The Open Secret

Statue! Don't move. Sit without moving.

When we say 'Statue', we mean sitting like an idol, unmoved. When you are sitting like an idol, you are learning the secret of being an idol. The secret of understanding something deeply is to become that thing yourself. You want to understand some emotion, then live in that emotion to understand it deeply. There are so many things in this universe, that can be known in their true essence only by becoming one with them.

Maha Shivaratri is an auspicious and perfect occasion to see how some things can be learnt in a different way, in an unconventional way. You came into the world unaware, but should not leave without knowing the Open Secret!

The Open Secret Of Shiva

Without knowing and understanding this secret, all your prayers and offerings will be wasted. The benefits that you hope and expect, will remain unattainable to you. You need to first learn the Open Secret to attain true fulfillment in life.

In order to understand the Open Secret, you need to know its real meaning and apply it in your life without getting stuck in words. Words are being used here to convey only the Open Secret and nothing else. Only those words are useful that can help you in understanding the Open Secret. Otherwise, they are useless even if they are taken from the *Shastras*, Vedas or religious scriptures.

To understand the Open Secret, you need to be in a receptive frame. It helps to develop a stillness and be seated like a statue to be able to absorb the essence of the message.

Why is it called 'Open' as well as 'Secret'? If it is a secret, then how can it be open?

Some things are so open, elaborate, and obvious that we are completely unaware of them. We completely miss them, even though they stare at us in the eye! Are we so ignorant that something is in front of us and we cannot see it! Let's understand this with an analogy.

Finding The Chocolate

You are asked to go into a huge mansion to fetch a chocolate from an old cupboard in the dining room. Now you enter the mansion and find the old cupboard. It has a lot of shelves; you open every drawer and search every corner of all the shelves. But you don't find the chocolate.

You then look around everywhere in the mansion, even in other cupboards, but find nothing. Dejected, you come out and declare that there was no chocolate to be found in that mansion. You blame the one who asked you to go and find it, saying that he was making a fool of you.

Then the one, who asked you to get the chocolate, generously reveals the Open Secret! As soon as you get to know the Open Secret, you are stunned. What do you learn?

You realize that the whole cupboard was made of chocolate! Look at the skilled craftsmanship! The entire cupboard was made of chocolate and you were looking inside it for a small bar of chocolate.

You are told to go back and look again. Equipped with this revelation of the Open Secret, you now know things differently and of course, your way of looking at the cupboard has also changed.

So when you are sent back to the mansion again, you will be astounded at what you see. You come back exclaiming that it is not just the cupboard, but the entire mansion – its walls, furniture… everything is made of chocolate!

Now the joy that you experience is not due to the fact that you know that the cupboard is made of chocolate. You are finding joy in the fact that you are able to know the profoundness of the Open Secret at a deeper level. Just seeing the Open Secret revealed before your eyes can become the cause of unspeakable bliss!

But if your happiness is because you have a mansion-sized chocolate to eat, then you have missed the essence of the secret totally.

How could you have missed it! You then realize that you had assumed the chocolate to come in a certain wrapper. You expected to see some known chocolate brand. You also realize that you were looking for it at a fixed place, assuming that it can't be elsewhere. So you were missing what was so very obvious all the time.

What did you understand from this analogy? What is it that is present right in front of your eyes in plain sight, everywhere, all the time, which you don't see?

The Shiva, the true Self that you seek, is bringing everything alive. It touches every aspect of life – from the mundane to the extraordinary, from the painful to the most pleasurable. Shiva is the conscious essence of every moment that you are alive. Yet you miss it, because you seek it in the wrappers of concepts and the brands of ideologies!

After coming to know the Open Secret, what will be your perspective when you go back into the world? Your perspective would undergo a paradigm shift!

But wait, there is more to it. When you come and express your wonder about what you have found, the one who asked you to find the chocolate has an enigmatic smile. He then reveals the complete secret!

And what is the complete secret? He reveals that YOU are the chocolate that you were trying to find!

All this while, you believed in searching for what can give you true and lasting happiness and fulfillment. And now it is revealed to you that you *are* fulfillment itself! You are already the happiness that you seek. You, essentially are the love that you seek out. You are the Peace that you are constantly looking for. You just need to be with yourself to realize all of this.

If this is truly grasped, then it can be a Eureka moment in your life!

People can be easily satisfied with very little. The most that happens is that people find the small chocolate and feel immediately contented. They look at the sky, yet are unable to see its vastness; they can at best see clouds, birds, stars, the sun and the moon. They are easily satisfied with trivial little things.

People go searching for secrets of Shiva, find a few of things and are contented with those. There are seekers who come from far off countries to India to learn about Shaivism. What is it all about and what are the secrets behind its mythology? They read books about it, explore it thoroughly, and understand a few things. They just touch the surface of the information, but are contented with that alone, believing that they know it all now! They are happy with just one chocolate and leave contented.

Meaning Of Bhabhoot

Let's understand the meaning of *Bhabhoot* – the holy ash that Shiva and his devotees smear on their body.

Many people associate the feeling of fear with the way Shiva is depicted. The smearing of ash on the body, the Rudra Tandav dance and names like *Kaal Bhairav* cause disgust and fear in some people. There are also others, who accept these symbols and practices on their face value. These latter kind of people want to stand out in a crowd and will do any kind of stunts, just to show that they are better off than others. They will insert needles in their bodies, eat live cockroaches; just to gain public appreciation and to prove that they are performing feats that other people would normally avoid. People start either respecting them or despising them for their bizzarre feats. Hence, these feats become a trendy thing to do.

But the Open Secret was not meant for these things.

When the Open Secret starts disappearing, people catch hold a part of it and convert it into a ritual, and present themselves as gurus or spiritual masters. The presentation is done in such a way that the task seems very unique and special, and the common man does not have the capability of doing it.

In India, anyone can project a talisman as a spiritual key containing miraculous powers. Anybody can don saffron robes and make predictions, becoming a self-proclaimed Guru. It has become a child's play to behave in a spiritual manner and others respect them unconditionally.

Since everyone is looking for happiness, they will believe any conman to hand them their happiness with nonsense talk and rituals. But this is not spirituality. Even those things that are not associated with Shiva become attached to Him. That is how the real knowledge is lost along the way while pretentious, make-believe talk is left.

Now you can see how irrelevant things have gained importance, and what is the real truth. Let's move on, equipped with this information.

Why does Shiva apply the bhabhoot all over his body? People don't know the real reason for smearing the *bhasm* on the body. What does it indicate?

'*Bha*' stands for the future (*Bhavishya*), '*bhoot*' stands for the past. 'Bhavishya-bhoot-bhasm'. The holy ash of the Past-and-Future.

Smearing the holy ash is a symbol of burning the past and future and atoning for your sins. You don't need to visit a cremation or burial grounds in order to achieve this. You can work to be free from your past and future even sitting at home. The ash is only a symbol.

When you are free from the pull of the past and future, then you can remain focused in the present. The present is where you can consciously plant the seeds for your future through the thoughts that you choose, through the feelings that you keep. So you sit in the present, having burnt the past and future. Applying bhabhoot denotes that.

The Place Of Shiva In The Holy Trinity

People commonly speak of the Holy Trinity of Brahma, Vishnu and Mahesh as the creator, preserver, and destroyer of the universe. But then, where is Shiva positioned in this trinity?

In order to understand this, let us explore the mythological narrative of Lord Shiva's original state and understand its essential meaning.

Before the creation of the Universe, when Lord Brahma opened his eyes to look around, He saw nothing else but a Lotus flower. He asked, "Who am I?" So, Lord Brahma was the first seeker of truth in this Universe!

He was filled with questions about Himself, about His origin and why He was seated on the Lotus flower. He was curious about the flower's origin and how it was standing. Like any other seeker of truth, He kept searching for answers, but to no avail.

The seeker keeps searching for answers all the time. He reads books, meets people, contemplates deeply; the search is endless.

So the story goes that Lord Brahma met Lord Vishnu. The first living being that Lord Brahma saw was Lord Vishnu. He now asked the second question, "Who are you?" This is how relationships develop when you ask questions like "Who am I" and "Who are you".

When Lord Vishnu asked Lord Brahma the same question, he replied that He had created this world and therefore He must have created Lord Vishnu as well, along with the world. Lord Vishnu replied, "Oh… so you created me! But just look at where you have come from!"

Now you all know that the Lotus arises from Lord Vishnu's navel – that's why He is called *Padma-nabha*. And Lord Brahma was sitting on the same lotus and asking questions to Lord Vishnu!

What a deep thought this is, which cannot be explained simply! Who came first and who created whom? It's like the riddle of the chicken and the egg – what came first! This is an extremely puzzling question, that has been asked over the ages and yet the answer eludes people.

Likewise, it is difficult to ascertain who came first because Lord Brahma was created from Lord Vishnu's navel, but Lord Brahma created Lord Vishnu when He was creating the world.

We need to understand this analogy, because it is deeply related to our existence. If you don't understand the puzzle of the chicken and egg, it does not matter. It is not a crucial existential question beyond the understanding of the normal intellect. But it is necessary to solve the Brahma and Vishnu puzzle. Who created whom?

Eventually, both the Lords, Brahma and Vishnu, argued about the truth behind their origin. Lord Brahma is considered the Lord of Creation. He has created the universe and all the living beings in it, while Lord Vishnu is the Preserver of this universe.

As they were arguing, suddenly a tall pillar appeared in between them. The pillar extended infinitely from below the earth till the sky. Its upper and lower ends couldn't be seen at all. You could call that pillar the 'Shivaling'. It had a fire burning within it without any fuel.

We all know about the sun, that it is burning now, but it will end at some point in thousands of years. Even that is not limitless burning, but the fire within this pillar seemed to be self-fueling, without the need for any other fuel; it burns endlessly. That is why, Shiva is also known as *Swayambhu* or *Shambhu*, which means something that appears on its own, without a cause.

Now, when Lord Vishnu and Lord Brahma saw this massive pillar in the middle of nowhere, They decided that whoever would find one end of the pillar would be considered as the superior God. Lord Brahma decided to become a swan and fly up in the sky to locate the upper end while Lord Vishnu became a white boar that burrowed into the earth to unearth the lower end of the pillar.

Both of them kept searching and it was endless. The pillar was limitless. While Lord Brahma was flying high, He found some leaves and *Ketki* flowers that could have been offerings to the Shivaling. But He couldn't see the upper end. Both the Gods returned, having failed in Their mission.

Despite this, Lord Brahma bragged that He had seen the top end, since He had seen the flowers and leaves. Lord Vishnu believed Him.

But then, Lord Shiva appeared all of a sudden. He was angry with Lord Brahma for lying and manipulating the facts. He then cursed Him. Lord Shiva said that although Lord Brahma was part of the Holy Trinity, He will not be worshipped by humanity.

Was Lord Shiva justified in cursing Lord Brahma? He had to be right, because a person gains eligibility for wisdom through sincerity and honesty, and not through deceit.

Lord Brahma had lied, merely to gain superiority over Lord Vishnu. Although He did create the world, yet he is not worshipped for it. Barring one or two, you will not find temples of Lord Brahma in the world. If at all there are, it is to prove the point that by using deceit you cannot gain importance, even if you are part of the Holy Trinity. Everyone is equal, yet if they use dishonest or deceitful means, they will be admonished. They will be cursed.

In today's world, it is not that Shiva personally comes to curse you if you have been resorting to corrupt practices. If you have been deceitful in proving your eligibility, like a curse, your knowledge will not come in handy at crucial times when you need it the most.

In the Mahabharata, Karna attained knowledge through deceitful means and was admonished by his Guru Lord Parashurama. When he needed it the most in the battle, his skills and prowess could not come to his rescue.

What people fail to understand is that if Lord Brahma could have become the recipient of such a curse due to a single deceit, then it is possible for ordinary people too.

See how it has been portrayed in the story. Even though all three of them are part of the Holy Trinity, Lord Brahma is excluded from worship, because of His dishonesty. This trial was done to convey the importance of truthfulness and honesty.

We need to contemplate on this and consider all the possible times when we may have even remotely indulged in wrong practices to gain something. It is a good time to seek forgiveness for all your misgivings, so that you can start afresh in your search and attainment of eligibility for wisdom.

The Open Secret of Shiva is beyond the grasp of the human intellect. The three Gods, Lord Brahma, Lord Vishnu and Lord Mahesh, are all visible, but you cannot see Shiva amidst them. This is the Open Secret, which is beyond comprehension, because we have seen pictures of the Holy Trinity, but we have never noticed that Shiva is *not* there!

Why is Shiva not seen in the Holy Trinity

Now let us look at why Lord Shiva is not seen in the Holy Trinity.

There are three gurus, who travel together everywhere to spread knowledge. People approach them with their questions. All three are there to bless mankind.

What people don't know is that one of them is the real Guru, while the other two are disciples. Nobody was aware of this secret and since they always went together and blessed people, it did not matter who the Guru was and who the disciples were. They were giving their blessings and that was the bottom line of prime importance.

But the disciples knew who the Guru was. Lord Brahma and Lord Vishnu, both knew that Lord Shiva had emerged as the Shivaling that appeared between them.

Legend has it that Shiva had ten hands and five heads, with each head having a third eye. So, in total, he had fifteen eyes including five third eyes! All this is symbolic. There is a reason for such a detailed description of Shiva. It is to depict his capacity and capabilities with fifteen eyes and ten hands. It was necessary to give a visual for Shiva's appearance, because people can visually understand the truths better.

The Shivaling was used to give it a formless description, but then people added eyes to it! Without a form, it becomes difficult for people to worship and that is why they gave Shiva physical features. The disciples were aware of who the Guru among them was.

Then one day, Lord Shiva decided to detach Himself from the universe and become invisible. He asked Lord Brahma to create His form and infuse it with life. Of those three, this was the specialty of Lord Brahma. He could breathe life into a dead idol. With this command, the Principal Guru, the Adi-Guru, vanished and was replaced with an idol. Thereafter, Lord Mahesh came to life, also to be known as Rudra.

So, the secret of the Holy Trinity of Gods is clear. All three are still present; their work continues as before. Lord Shiva has been called the Adi-Guru, because He is the first Guru. This is the first secret of Shiva, the Open Secret – Lord Shiva became detached and invisible; yet His form is still visible in the Trinity of Gods.

Lord Brahma can be called Lord Shiva's creator in a sense, but actually He is not. Lord Brahma knows that He was deceitful, but it was just a one-time incident. He knows that although He created Lord Shiva's idol, yet He cannot claim his ownership over it.

The word 'ownership' is very important here.

Man has created things, but does he really own them? Can man confidently claim that he is the creator of his creation? We need to understand this feeling of ownership that might infuse us with pride sometimes. What really is it? Without knowing fully, man tends to give himself too much importance in terms of creations and errs in the process.

It is essential to make man realize his mistake. Lord Brahma erred once, but He learnt His lesson. We need to own up our mistakes and learn from them, seek forgiveness to clear the karmic repercussion. Only then can we truly make progress.

For example, a man assists in creating a centre for welfare of the needy. He commences the operations of this organization with the help of many people who team up with him.

Then comes the pride associated with creating the centre. The man starts feeling a sense of ownership over the centre. He regards himself as the creator of the centre. He makes the same mistake that Brahma had made.

He needs to remember that he might have helped in creating the centre, but he cannot claim ownership over it. He served as the medium for commencing the centre, just like Lord Brahma was the medium, working on Lord Shiva's instructions. Lord Shiva was the one who made it possible for Lord Brahma to create His form.

These are the little things that can entangle one in arrogance, that are to be avoided. The secret is to remain detached from words, especially titles and designations. Words can mislead you, causing false expectations and unnecessary pride.

When you look at the Holy Trinity, you cannot see Lord Shiva in it. Though He is present, He is invisible. His visible form is activated as Maheshwara; He is Maha-Ishwara – the Great God.

Forms are being created and destroyed. Brahma, Vishnu and Mahesh are active. But Lord Shiva, the original, the Adi-Guru is non-manifest. He is at rest as the silent background of everything.

God is the Generator, Operator and Destroyer. God-at-rest means the state of *Par Brahma*, the One who is beyond everything. That is the real Lord Shiva. But without a form, it is difficult for people to understand who Lord Shiva is. It is made somewhat easier for them to understand Lord Shiva through the Shivaling.

How beautiful these things are! If these stories had not been there, it would not have been possible to extend this knowledge to the next generation. A beautiful arrangement! But what generally happens at a later stage? People start misinterpreting these truths according to their own preferences and selfish agenda. In the process, the knowledge gets corrupted to such an extent that its original purpose is lost. It was meant to eradicate deceit, but unfortunately, people start using it to deceive others.

Whenever you see that knowledge is being misused, immediately remind yourself honestly and sincerely to adopt the right ways for yourself. Persevere to maintain your purity of mind, because it is then that the Ganga of Knowledge will flow in your life.

9
Being In The Flow Of Life

We desire things that we do not possess. A predominant thought that consumes most of us is: What do I do to get it? We look around at others who already possess what we desire and keep wondering how we can get it.

However, we can be free from such constant yearning that makes us feel incomplete. If we understand yet another secret of Shiva, we would be aware of the easier way.

There are three kinds of people in the world. Let us understand how they create things in their lives.

The Gong-man Uses Strength

The first kind of man sounds the gong. He is the Gong-man. He hits on a very big plate that creates a big sound that results in powerful vibrations that spread everywhere. According to the frequency of the vibrations, various things are created.

So, the Gong-man hits the gong and the vibrations that ensue start creating. The clay lying close by starts molding itself into various objects – a statue, a living being, etc.

The vibrations arise, exist for a little while and then die down. And so does their creation. When a vibration starts, so does a creation with it. As long as the vibration continues, creation continues, but as soon as the vibration drops, the creation also stops. Very often, the vibration is not enough to complete the thing being created and creation stops midway, leaving the scene incomplete.

When do you know that something has entered your life? Only when you see it in your life.

Suppose that you have wanted to get a television home since a very long time. A few days back you had rung the gong that you want to watch colorful films, for which you need a color TV set. To get to the point where the TV reaches your house and plays movies, the vibrations need to be sustained for some time.

People elevate their vibrations, but then bring them down soon, under the influence of illusory negative scenes. As soon as they see that things do not seem to be working out, they get disappointed and drop the vibration in between.

This is also the case with the desire for liberation. As soon as the vibration for attaining liberation starts, the thought comes, why do you need liberation? Liberation from what? Life is to enjoy! Enjoy what the world has to offer. Unfortunately, man doesn't know the meaning of enjoyment. He does not understand the joy of real freedom. But as soon as such thoughts occur to him, the auspicious vibration drops.

This is happening universally. Every human has a vibration going on inside them as soon as they rise up in the morning. These vibrations are the seeds of creation. If they are positive, they will manifest positivity. But if they are negative, they will manifest negativity. For example, when you enter the bathroom after getting up and find that there's no water supply; the tap is dry, you frown and grumble. The moment you frown, the vibration drops. The vibration that you take with you into the day will structure the future incidents of the day. Negative or positive fluctuations in your vibration will structure the incidents accordingly, setting the tone for your future.

When certain events seem to go against what people desire, they conclude that they cannot attain fulfilment. When things don't seem to be going as planned, doubts arise. These very doubts bring down the vibration that can manifest their aspirations.

There is also the vibration of 'Being', the inner sense of "havingness", which creates a feeling of gratitude that everything is happening, that everything is available. This vibration, though subtle, continues to work. But due to ignorance of this, people will always be greedy for more and keep struggling, thereby nullifying this vibration.

People, who are always concerned about their work remaining incomplete, will constantly worry about getting just a little more of everything to complete their tasks – a little more power, or information, or connections, a little more money, or a better or bigger place to live. The list is endless. There is always a need for something more. So they always live in the vibration of "lack", that there isn't enough. Ignorance of the truth of how life works makes people feel that if they gain something more, they will feel complete. It's like a mirage that they are chasing. On the contrary, it is the vibration you are in, the way you create, that is important.

If you are using the Gong-man's approach of brute strength to manifest what you wish in life, then it is bound to fail. Not everything can be obtained with force. It might have worked at some point earlier, but it doesn't work every time. People create success formulae, based on their past success patterns. And then they struggle to repeat the success through the same ways.

The limited mind is bound to believe that if it worked earlier, then there must be power in brute force, there must be power in your social status and position, and so on. This is only physical or muscle power. If a person has faith in brawn power, what does he do when he wants something? He snatches it from others.

On the other hand, what does a cunning person do in the same scenario? He distracts the other person and usurps the thing from the other person cleverly, without letting the person know about what was done. He uses his brain power. He feels that this is a better way of acquiring things, but he never realizes when this power of the mind becomes a curse!

There is no purity of mind! The moon on Shiva's head is a symbol of coolness, of purity of mind. The white snow on Mount Kailash is a symbol of calm and peace. But man lacks these qualities. He believes that he has acquired his possessions with his strength and power. However, soon this power becomes a curse. He uses his power to acquire things, but the arrogance that develops in the process brings suffering. The higher the position of power and responsibility, the greater the purity of mind is required.

A man starts practicing as a doctor. Soon, he starts making a name for himself and has a long queue of patients waiting at his clinic. The higher he goes in his status and recognition, the more important is purity of mind for him. Similarly, a tutor giving tuitions has a long queue of students waiting to learn from him; he too needs to have higher purity of mind.

Brawn or brain power can very soon turn into a curse. That is why, people with position and power should learn to be grateful for the skills, position, or possessions that they have. It is not necessary to become a Gong-man. Power must not corrupt your understanding and values. Otherwise, people become like Gong-men with the motto of 'Gong never goes wrong,' being filled with ego and arrogance.

With Gong-men, there is power that encourages employing more strength to create something new. The hunger for more power and strength keeps increasing. This is what leads to a life of constant struggle.

When your efforts come from a place of struggle, then you try to manifest your aspirations by force. Such forceful efforts only produce limited results. Are you using forceful efforts backed by will power?

Are you in a state of struggle? The results with this approach will not be sustainable.

Certain things do get created with such forceful effort. However, when people believe that "forceful doing" is the only way to achieve success, they see it as the only workable method and indulge in fierce competition due to the notion of scarcity. The notion of scarcity manifests only more scarcity.

Common Man Keeps Complaining

The second kind of people is the "Common man". He is weak and keeps complaining about everything that has happened with him. What does a weak man do when he wants something that others have? He can obviously not snatch it. So, he complains that he did not get what his heart desired.

He will complain about what others did, or what they did not do, and how everything hurts him so. This is so common! Life keeps moving for the common man, things do happen as desired, but he fails to notice the good things that are happening in his life. He lives and dies without learning the secret of how things are created in life.

Ganga-man Revels In The Flow Of The Ganga Of Knowledge

The third way is that of the Ganga-man. How is he made? He revels in the river of knowledge and flows in its waters. Metaphorically speaking, these people remain seated under the flow of the Ganga emanating from Lord Shiva and let it cascade over them. They sit down next to Shiva with open arms, absorbing the knowledge that is cascading from Lord Shiva.

They have received the Ganga; the river of knowledge is flowing and they have a firm grip on it. So then, what is their way of creating things in their lives? It is not the way of the weak, or of the complainer, or the gong-men.

You can choose any of the ways discussed. But people will not choose the first way, because they know that strength involves a lot of struggle. Man carries unnecessary resistance within him. The second way was that of the common man. That is also not a preferred choice. The highest choice is the third one, the way of the Ganga-man.

Meditation To Practice The Way Of The Ganga-man

To understand the way of the Ganga-man, let's consider a meditation. You may record these instructions in your voice and play them whenever you want to practice it.

Be seated in a comfortable posture. Close your eyes and raise your hands up in the air. Imagine that the knowledge of Ganga is flowing from Lord Shiva and you are seated down next to him, to absorb this transcendental knowledge.

Hands open and raised, eyes closed. Let the waters of understanding cascade down upon you. The more the water pours on you, the more the whiteness increases. You move into a meditative trance. You are in a receptive state, allowing the highest knowledge to pour over your hands into your body.

Take relaxed breaths, slowly. Breathe in the flow of wisdom and let out all resistance with a feeling of gratitude. Sit peacefully and enjoy each breath as it comes in and goes out. As you relax, the expression of gratitude keeps becoming purer. Initially, it may seem an effort, but subsequently, the feeling of gratitude arises effortlessly.

Look within yourself; see the entire world within – the globe, the country, the state, the district, the city, your locality, and the place you're seated. Imagine everything to be painted white, inside as well as on the outside.

Now check all the vehicles on the road – white car, white motorbike, white bicycle – they are also all white. People are roaming around in these white vehicles and so are you. Even the clothing is white, from head to the shoes. Everything is white.

If everything is turning to white, it means everything is disappearing, because nobody and nothing is standing out. There is no contrast of color, indicating that the world is dissolving in the whiteness.

Showering under the waterfall, under the white free-flowing water that is fresh and pure, you are in a mode of total acceptance. You are learning the third way – the way of the Ganga-man.

Tell yourself, "Whatever comes to me, should come smoothly in a free-flow, just like this waterfall. I am open and inviting it to fully bathe me. Be it health, skills, wealth, relationships, love, happiness and peace; everything is flowing in the grace of Ganga. I am just present in this divine flow. All problems are getting washed away, all disease that are visible or hidden within me are getting washed away in the free-flowing waters of the Ganga."

Place your hands on your lap. Everything will return back to normal. You may open your eyes now.

In Free flow

During the meditation, you were symbolically seated under the flowing waters of the Ganga in a receptive mode, willing to absorb everything that was flowing into your life. You experienced what it actually means to bathe in the Ganga.

People visit Haridwar and Kashi to take a dip in the holy waters of the Ganga. But many lack this understanding of the importance of bathing in the pure, sacred and free flow.

But, through this meditation, you have taken a brief dip into the experience of being seated in an open and welcoming mental posture, ready to absorb everything that is coming your way in life.

You just need to be in the free-flow. Things are coming to you naturally. This is the beauty of this way, this flow of Ganga. You wanted relations to improve, and you now have the key to harmony in relationships. You wanted financial independence; you have the ultimate way of welcoming abundance in your life.

You wanted joy and peace; you now know the way of being in joy and peace and allowing creation to happen! In the third way of the Ganga-man, you learn the art of 'being there', just being present in the flow of life.

As soon as you feel any form of resistance arising within you, remind yourself of this message – "I just need to be present in an open state and welcome the free-flow into my life. Whatever is mine will naturally come to me. Nothing or nobody can take it away."

The flow of Ganga is the flow of life. It is continuous, fulfilling the entire world's wishes, washing away everyone's sins and removing all disease. People just need to learn to 'be there'.

The common man is weak and helpless and therefore ends up resorting to backbiting, complaining and blaming others. But as soon as he understands the right approach, he realizes how futile it is to be negative and blame others for his problems. It becomes clear to him that there is no need to adopt negative ways of acquiring things in life. Everything would come on its own to him, at the right time.

Satisfaction Within

The more you practice living in receptivity to the free-flow of life, your confidence in the efficacy of this approach will increase. You will practically see everything coming to you easily.

Then comes the next step that will lead you beyond this stage. Bathing in the river of free-flow, being in the Ganga of life, is self-satisfying, self-fulfilling in itself. Everything else, all other achievements are merely a bonus.

Are those people who have achieved a lot in life, fully satisfied with their lives? You may find that most aren't. They remain discontented all through their lives and die without completeness. When Alexander was asked what would he do next after winning over the entire world, he kept searching for the answer! He went into a fit of depression with this question. He had achieved everything by brute force. He had conquered lands far beyond Greece. But he hadn't found self-satisfaction; he hadn't arrived home!

You gain self-contentment by being seated in the free-flow of life, where you discover the true meaning of being happy. Actually, being happy is your true nature.

Once this is understood, the desire for anything else ends. Then whatever comes to you is a bonus. You will be rid of the emotions of jealousy, complaining, comparing with others and yearning for what others have. You will no longer care for the make-believe, artificiality in the world.

When you exist in the free-flow of life, equipped with this understanding, being empty-handed does not distress you anymore. There might be times when you are sitting under the flow with your arms stretched out, expecting something to come your way. But nothing does. Don't get depressed; on the contrary, translate the experience into positive outcomes.

The Trident of three magics

When things don't seem to be happening as you would have wished, just remember the words, "Let Thy will be mine." "Let the divine will play out as it wishes in my life." As soon as you say these words, your attention will move from the pain and you begin to move ahead. You won't remain stuck with your painful emotions.

When you surrender to the divine will, to the divine flow of life, your focus automatically shifts from your empty hands to the free-flow of abundance.

When seemingly negative situations appear, there are three types of magic which will help you. What are these?

The magic of acceptance, the magic of patience, and the magic of conscious self-talk. Whenever you fall out of the flow of Ganga, you need to remember these three. They are the trident – the Trishul – that you see Lord Shiva wielding in His hand. You need to absorb them and adapt them to your lifestyle.

With the magic of acceptance, you can do away with all resistance that the mind holds to situations in life. With the magic of patience, you can be calm when you see your hands empty; when things are not happening in time as you would expect. When you shift your focus from lack to the abundant flow, you will be surprised to see things getting created expeditiously. With the magic of conscious self-talk, you can guide your thoughts to focus on the free-flow by consciously choosing your words, instead of getting entangled in the web of negative illusion.

Whatever you wanted – the qualities, the kind of work you wished to do; you will find it all. But the real joy will also come, when you learn to abide in the source of happiness within you. You will begin to be happy just because you exist!

A lot of people believe in putting their wishes in the 'magic box' and leaving it up to God to fulfill them. Then they release their wishes. Many a times, they may even forget and realize it much later that plenty of their wishes have already been fulfilled. We may not even remember our wishes, yet they were granted to us. Therefore, we need to learn this magic.

Be in the free-flow of life and allow life to happen naturally, spontaneously.

■■■

You can send your opinion or feedback on this book to :

Tej Gyan Foundation, Pimpri Colony, P. O. Box 25,
Pimpri, Pune – 411017 (Maharashtra), INDIA
email : mail@tejgyan.com

Write for Us

We welcome writers, translators and editors to join our team. If you would like to volunteer, please email us at: englishbooks@tejgyan.org or call : +91 90110 10963

About Sirshree

(Symbol of Acceptance)

Sirshree's spiritual quest which began during his childhood, led him on a journey through various schools of thought and meditation practices. His overpowering desire to attain the truth made him relinquish his teaching job. After a long period of contemplation, his spiritual quest culminated in the attainment of the ultimate truth. Sirshree says, **"All paths that lead to the truth begin differently, but end in the same way—with understanding. Understanding is the whole thing. Listening to this understanding is enough to attain the truth."**

Sirshree is the author of several spiritual books. His books have been translated in more than 10 languages and published by leading publishers such as Penguin and Hay House. He is the founder of Tej Gyan Foundation, a not-for-profit organization committed to raising mass consciousness by spreading "Happy Thoughts" with branches in the United States, India, Europe and Asia-Pacific. Sirshree's retreats have transformed the lives of thousands and his teachings have inspired various social initiatives for raising global consciousness.

His works include more than 100 books and 3000 discourses. Various luminaries and celebrities such as His Holiness the Dalai Lama, publishers Mr. Reid Tracy and Ms. Tami Simon and yoga master Dr. B. K. S Iyengar have released Sirshree's books and lauded his work. 'The Source' book series, authored by Sirshree, has sold more than 10 million copies in 5 years. His book *The Warrior's Mirror*, published by Penguin, was featured in the Limca Book of Records for being released on the same day in 11 languages.

Tejgyan... The Road Ahead

What is Tejgyan?

Tejgyan is the existential wisdom of the ultimate truth, which is beyond duality. In today's world, there are people who feel disharmony and are desperately trying to achieve balance in an unpredictable life. Tejgyan helps them in harmonizing with their true nature, the Self, thereby restoring balance in all aspects of their life.

And then there are those who are successful but feel a sense of emptiness or void within. Tejgyan provides them fulfillment and helps them to embark on a journey towards self-realization. There are others who feel lost and are seeking the meaning of life. Tejgyan helps them to realize the true purpose of human life.

All this is possible with Tejgyan due to a very simple reason. The experience of the ultimate truth is always available. The direct experience of this truth is possible provided the right method is known. Tejgyan is that method, that understanding. At Tej Gyan Foundation, Sirshree imparts this understanding through a System for Wisdom – a series of retreats that guides participants step by step

Magic of Ultimate Awakening Retreat

Magic of Ultimate Awakening is the flagship self-realization retreat offered by Tej Gyan Foundation The retreat is conducted in two languages – Hindi and English. The teachings of the retreat are non-denominational (secular).

This residential retreat is held for 3-5 days at the foundation's MaNaN Ashram amidst the glory of mountains and the pristine beauty of nature. This ashram is located at the outskirts of the city of Pune in India, and is well connected by air, road and rail. The retreat is also held at other centres of Tej Gyan Foundation across the world.

Participate in the *Magic of Ultimate Awakening* retreat to attain ageless wisdom through a unique simple 'System for Wisdom' so that you can:

1. Live from pure and still presence allowing the natural qualities of consciousness, viz. peace, love, joy, compassion, abundance and creativity to manifest.
2. Acquire simple tools to use in everyday life which help quieten the chattering mind, revealing your true nature.
3. Get practical techniques to access pure presence at will and connect to the source of all answers (the inner guru).
4. Discover missing links in practices of meditation *(dhyana)*, action *(karma)*, wisdom *(gyana)* and devotion *(bhakti)*.
5. Understand the nature of your body-mind mechanism to attain freedom from tendencies and patterns.
6. Learn practical methods to shift from mind-centred living to consciousness-centred living.

For retreats, contact +919921008060 or email: mail@tejgyan.com

A Mini retreat is also conducted, especially for teens (14-17 years) during summer and winter vacations

MaNaN Ashram

Survey No. 43, Sanas Nagar, Nandoshi gaon, Kirkatwadi Phata, Sinhagad Road, Dist. Pune 411024, Maharashtra, India.

About Tej Gyan Foundation

Tej Gyan Foundation (TGF) was established with the mission of creating a highly evolved society through all-round self development of every individual that transforms all the facets of his/her life. It is a non-profit organization founded on the teachings of Sirshree. The foundation has received the ISO certification (ISO 9001:2015) for its system of imparting wisdom. It has centres all across India as well as in other countries. The motto of Tej Gyan Foundation is 'Happy Thoughts'.

TGF is creating a highly evolved society through:

1. Tejgyan Programs (Retreats, Courses, Television and Radio Programs, Podcasts)

2. Tejgyan Products (Books, Tapes, Audio/Video CDs)

3. Tejgyan Projects (Value Education, Women Empowerment, Peace Initiatives)

TGF undertakes projects to elevate the level of consciousness among students, youth, women, senior citizens, teachers, doctors, leaders, organizations, police force, prisoners, etc.

Now you can register **online** for the following retreats

Maha Aasmani Param Gyan Shivir
(5 Days Residential Retreat in Hindi)

Magic of Ultimate Awakening Retreat
(3 Days Residential Retreat In English)

Mini Maha Aasmani Shivir
3 Days (Residential) Retreat for Teens

🔍 www.tejgyan.org

Books can be delivered at your doorstep by registered post or courier. You can request for the same through postal money order or pay by VPP. Please send the money order to any one of the following two addresses:

WOW Publishings Pvt. Ltd.

1. Registered Office: E-4, Vaibhav Nagar, Near Tapovan Mandir, Pimpri, Pune - 411017

2. Post Box No.36, Pimpri Colony Post Office, Pimpri, Pune - 411017

Phone No.: 9011013210 / 9623457873

You can also order your copy at the online store:
www.gethappythoughts.org

*Free Shipping plus 10% Discount on purchases above Rs. 300/-

For further details contact:
Tejgyan Global Foundation
Registered Office:

Happy Thoughts Building, Vikrant Complex, Near Tapovan Mandir, Pimpri, Pune 411017, Maharashtra, India.
Contact No: 020-27411240, 27412576
Email: mail@tejgyan.com

MaNaN Ashram:
Survey No. 43, Sanas Nagar, Nandoshi gaon, Kirkatwadi Phata, Sinhagad Road, Tal. Haveli, Dist. Pune 411024, Maharashtra, India.
Contact No: 992100 8060.

Hyderabad: 9885558100, **Bangalore:** 9880412588, **Delhi:** 9891059875, **Nashik:** 9326967980, **Mumbai:** 9373440985

For accessing our unique 'System for Wisdom' from self-help to self-realization, please follow us on:

	Website	www.tejgyan.org
	Video Channel	www.youtube.com/tejgyan For Q&A videos: http://goo.gl/YA81DQ
	Social networking	www.facebook.com/tejgyan
	Social networking	www.twitter.com/sirshree
	Internet Radio	http://www.tejgyan.org/internetradio.aspx

Online Shopping
www.gethappythoughts.org

Pray for World Peace along with thousands of others
at 09:09 a.m. and p.m. every day

www.ingramcontent.com/pod-product-compliance
Lightning Source LLC
LaVergne TN
LVHW041844070526
838199LV00045BA/1424